Trip Sheets

Ellen Hawley

MILKWEED EDITIONS

The characters and events in this book are fictitious. Any similarity to real persons, living or dead, is coincidental and not intended by the author.

© 1998, Text by Ellen Hawley
© 1998, Cover painting by Matthew Madson
All rights reserved. Except for brief quotations in critical articles or reviews, no part of this book may be reproduced in any manner without prior written permission from the publisher: Milkweed Editions, 430 First Avenue North, Suite 400, Minneapolis, MN 55401
Distributed by Publishers Group West

Published 1998 by Milkweed Editions
Printed in the United States of America
Cover design by Gail Wallinga
Cover art by Matthew Madson
Interior design by Wendy Holdman
The text of this book is set in Cochin.
98   99   00   01   02   5   4   3   2   1
First Edition

Milkweed Editions is a not-for-profit publisher. We gratefully acknowledge support from the Elmer L. and Eleanor J. Anderson Foundation; James Ford Bell Foundation; Dayton's, Mervyn's, and Target Stores by the Dayton Hudson Foundation; Doherty, Rumble and Butler Foundation; Dorsey and Whitney Foundation; Ecolab Foundation; General Mills Foundation; Honeywell Foundation; Hubbard Foundation; Jerome Foundation; McKnight Foundation; Minnesota State Arts Board through an appropriation by the Minnesota State Legislature; Challenge and Creation and Presentation Programs of the National Endowment for the Arts; Lawrence and Elizabeth Ann O'Shaughnessy Charitable Income Trust in honor of Lawrence M. O'Shaughnessy; Oswald Family Foundation; Piper Jaffray Companies, Inc.; Ritz Foundation on behalf of Mr. and Mrs. E. J. Phelps, Jr.; John and Beverly Rollwagen Fund of the Minneapolis Foundation; St. Paul Companies, Inc.; Star Tribune/Cowles Media Foundation; Surdna Foundation; James R. Thorpe Foundation; and generous individuals.

Library of Congress Cataloging-in-Publication Data

Hawley, Ellen.
  Trip sheets / Ellen Hawley. — 1st ed.
     p. cm.
  ISBN 1-57131-021-5 (paper)
  I. Title
PS3558.A82335T75   1998
813'.54—dc21   98-21809
                                                                        CIP

This book is printed on acid-free paper.

*For Ida
and for Jane and Peter*

Acknowledgments

"Men She Likes Otherwise" and "Beginning" first appeared in the *Threepenny Review*. "Comfort" first appeared in *In the Family*. "Distant Touch" first appeared in *American Voices: Webs of Diversity*.

I owe thanks to many people, but especially — for their encouragement, criticism, concrete information, concentrated goodwill, and existence — to Therese Cain, Claire Jordan, Nan Kane, Patrice Clark Koelsch, Julie Landsman, Jim Moore, Ellen Myre, Elizabeth Delza Munson, Danielle Pryor, Jan Rachel, Ida Swearingen, and Jane Whitledge. I'm indebted to Kay Ruane for a fine story that provided the impetus for my story "Beginning"; to Larry Williams, who sat in my cab on a couple of slow days and read some of his wonderful poems and part of a story, bringing me to the stunning realization that writing is created by living human beings; to the *Threepenny Review* for publishing the earliest pieces of this manuscript; to the Blue Moon and Seward cafes for being the next best thing to a writers' colony and for making a damn good cup of tea besides; to the Cabrini House transitional housing program and its residents and staff, who let me hang around and found something useful for me to do; to the Loft for making Minnesota a better place to be a writer than it would be otherwise, and to the people I've worked with there over the years; and to Emilie Buchwald for her thoughtful editing.

Contents

Men She Likes Otherwise — *3*
The Rules — *13*
Becoming a Frog — *17*
Half the Risks — *28*
Women — *35*
An Antidote to History — *37*
Starting Badly — *45*
The Evolution of Flying Squirrels — *49*
Stepping into the Air — *66*
Change — *76*
Résumé — *86*
The Part of This Moment That Isn't Hers — *88*
Starting Over — *96*
Ice — *98*
The Force of Gravity — *102*
Success Story — *115*
Opening — *122*
More Women — *124*
Words like a Stone — *128*
Beginning — *132*
Other People's Sins — *140*
Throwing Money Away — *151*
Getting It Right — *155*

Atoms, Molecules — *158*
Distant Touch — *173*
Unfinished Dreams — *196*
Evening — *201*
Seven Things — *204*
Comfort — *220*

Trip Sheets

Men She Likes Otherwise

It's a little before noon when Cath pulls her cab into the garage and slams the key down in front of Warren.

"A drunk just peed in the back seat, I'm going home, and if anyone feels like firing me I'm all for it," she says.

Warren laughs.

"It'll dry. Be glad you don't drive nights."

Cath makes a face and stalks into the drivers' room. This is separated from the rest of the garage by three-quarter walls, and at this time of day it's empty. Standing under a sign that says, "Drivers MAY NOT draw more than 20% of their earnings," she totals her trip sheet on a calculator that someone's glued to the counter. She's made her share of jokes about the company being so cheap it has to glue down a five-dollar calculator, but she knows that if it weren't glued down, it would be gone. She's thought about prying it up herself. Not because she wants a calculator, but because it's the company's. And because it's glued down.

She figures twenty percent to the penny even though she doesn't need the cash, even though she manages better when she turns her money in and waits for a paycheck. It's easier than prying up the calculator, and less risky. She pulls money out of the pockets of her jeans, flattens it, and begins to count, turning the bills so they face up. No one's ever told her why cab drivers do this, or even that she should, but by now she'd feel unprofessional if she turned her money in helter-skelter.

She's folding the company's money into the envelope when Warren comes in and leans against the wall.

Warren doesn't quite fit as a cab driver. He should be selling something. Real estate, or photocopiers. Cath assumes he's a casualty of the recession, but she's never asked about it. He's wearing a white shirt, and it stands out like a flag against the grayness of the garage. Eventually they'll make him a dispatcher, or a regular supervisor instead of a substitute, and he'll tell himself initiative really is rewarded.

"I ever tell you what happened to me when I drove dog shift?" he says.

She pours the coins into the envelope and seals it.

"I don't want to hear about it."

She hands him the envelope without pausing, without meeting his eye, and stalks across the garage, aware that he's stepped out of the drivers' room and is watching her, aware that Rod, the mechanic, is leaning against his workbench and watching her over the rim of his thermos cup. Her rubber soles scrape softly against the cement, and her walk feels stiff and unnatural.

"Don't let it get to you," Warren calls after her when she's almost at the open door.

"Why the hell shouldn't I?" she yells over her shoulder. She hears him laugh, then she's squinting in the sunlight, and even though she's still in Warren's line of sight her walk becomes her own again.

Her car's parked across the street, in front of the North Port Vending office, in full sun. When she unlocks it, the heat rolls out, thick and stifling. She leans against it, waiting for it to cool a bit. She doesn't want to get in, doesn't want to go home, doesn't want to figure out what to do with the rest of the day, although she has half a dozen things she should be doing.

It was not wanting to go home that led her to sleep with Warren a few months ago. She was between quarters at the U and went out for a drink after work with a group of drivers. When the others started to drift home, Warren noticed her reluctance and bought another round. He was easy to drink with, he didn't push her, and they ended up at his place. He's been friendlier since then, and she hasn't wanted to be within thirty feet of him.

She drives home and begins the ritual that never quite cleanses her of a day's driving: She takes her shoes off, throws them at the opposite wall, and runs a brush through her hair. The brush catches in the snarls and pulls at her scalp, dragging some small part of the day's meanness out. She splashes water on her face and leans on the sink, water dripping from her chin. Then she picks her shoes up and sets them side by each in the closet.

When she's done, she sits at the table and makes a list of things she can't do with her life anymore.

Drive cab, she writes.

She looks out the window onto Northern Avenue. The light turns green, releasing a stream of cars.

Sleep with men I don't like, she writes.

Sleep with men I like otherwise.

She looks down onto Northern again. The light turns red, cutting off the traffic. Two teenage boys walk past. She can't hear their words, but their voices are high and angry. They're pissed off at someone, at something. They're teaching themselves how anger can fuel their lives. The light turns green, the traffic breaks loose, and the boys' voices go under.

She draws a line halfway down the page and starts a second list, things she could do instead.

Wait tables, she writes.

Drive school bus.

Actually write that damn mystery.

Buy an S & L.

She doodles on the edge of the page: stars, spirals, three-dimensional boxes. On any other day, the idea of writing the mystery would be enough to hold her attention. It's been evolving at the back of her head ever since she started driving cab. She keeps a notebook of plot twists, character sketches, and scene fragments, waiting for the day she's done with school and has time again. Today, though, her mind skips off it like a stone.

Women, she writes.

She cuts the list out of her journal, leaving a jagged edge behind, and turns it face down on the table. The thought she hasn't written out fully is *Sleep with women,* and even the shorthand form feels dangerous. Who knows where it would surface if she left it bound into the journal. She doesn't have a candidate in mind, but it's not a new thought, and it's been coming to her more often lately, and more powerfully. Last month she drove a bartender to work at a women's bar, and the bartender invited her to stop by and have a drink after work. Cath extended her shift first by one run, then by another, until they finally called her in so the night driver could take the cab out. By then she was too tired to go anywhere. She still thinks about the bartender, though. Thinks about her fine, strong hands. Thinks about herself walking into the bar. Thinks about the bartender not remembering her.

Even face down, the list troubles her. She folds it, then folds it again and tucks it under the Swedish ivy. Then she opens her Social Work Practice textbook and begins to read.

The next day she goes back to work. Because her rent's due on the first, because tuition'll be due again in the fall, because she hates waiting tables. And cab driving has a grip on her. It's like smoking, like sleeping with men.

She rolls out of the garage listening to the dispatcher's silence. Summer's always slow. Except for business travelers and old ladies, people with money don't ride cabs in good weather. They drive, they fly, they stay home. Hell, maybe they're teleported. Maybe they don't exist at all except when it's pouring or below zero. As for the rest of the world, it's getting toward the end of the month. Whatever money there was is gone, and the next check isn't due for a week. She rests her elbow on the window, and the wind rushes up her sleeve. The dispatcher calls a stand downtown, someone answers, and it's quiet again.

She deadheads to the airport, where there's also

nothing moving. Twenty cabs stand baking on the cement. The dispatcher breaks his silence.

"Nothing on the board, drivers, nothing anywhere. Try to stay awake out there."

A couple of drivers walk down the cab line and disappear into the men's room. Several minutes later they still haven't come out, which means they're shooting craps. Cath walks down the line until she finds a couple of drivers playing tonk in a toothpaste green cab with INDEPENDENT CAB CO. stenciled on the side. All four doors stand open searching for a breeze. She climbs into the back seat to watch the game. The driver in the passenger seat, Mac, has runnels of sweat streaming down his face. The cards slap against the clipboard. Money moves back and forth. Mac tells the other driver, Tommy Emler, to start the damn cab up and run the air-conditioning.

"Too expensive," Tommy says. "I own this cab. Who you think buys my gas?"

Mac grunts and shuffles the cards.

"Use some of the money you're winning off me. Hell, we can sit in my cab if you're too cheap to use my money."

"You sit anywhere you want." Tommy raps the steering wheel with both hands. "This is my cab. I'm staying here."

Mac deals the cards.

"Man's so cheap he doesn't want to see someone else spend money," he says to Cath.

Tommy studies his cards as if none of this has anything to do with him. He has reddish brown skin, bony hands, a dry shirt. The heat doesn't seem to touch him. Sweat runs in a river between Cath's breasts, but some part of her is also standing apart, as if she's already quit driving and only wants to remember what it was all like.

It's two hours before she gets a run. Tommy's long gone, and Mac's cab has been at the front of the line for half an hour while drivers pulled around it. Mac's in a game farther back in line with the windows closed and the air conditioner blasting.

Cath's passenger is a businessman who reminds her of Warren, a man who thinks the doors should all fly open because he knows how to be friendly.

"Do you mind if I ask something personal?" he says.

"Yeah, actually. I do."

Cath can almost hear him in the back seat recalibrating his approach. There's a longish pause, but when he tries again, he's still upbeat.

"It's just that I'm not used to seeing a woman driver — a woman cab driver. Especially an attractive one."

Cath lays on the horn to honk a drifting car back into its own lane and yells "Asshole" out the window. It's her best cab-driver imitation, and she's gratified when the passenger stops trying to talk to her.

After work she runs into her downstairs neighbor, Dave, by the mailboxes, and he invites her in for a beer. They've done this a few times — drunk a beer, watched some TV. He tells her he went to Sears last night and bought their last air conditioner. They sit on his couch and talk about air conditioners, about whether the earth's really getting warmer, and after a while she runs a finger across his wrist. His eyebrows rise like a question mark. He has black eyebrows, black hair that falls like water across his forehead.

She runs the finger up the inside of his arm and says, "Why shouldn't we?"

He brushes her hand uncertainly, then kisses her. By the time they're struggling with each other's buttons, she knows it's not a good idea. He's one of the men she likes otherwise; it doesn't carry over to this. When he takes his shirt off, he's modeling an appendectomy scar. She runs a finger along it, which turns out not to be a sexy gesture, although she meant it to be. She kisses the scar, hoping one or the other of them will do something to make it all fall into place, but neither of them does, and they make a dry, predictable kind of love, then crunch the pillows against the wall so they can sit side by side. The air conditioner grinds out cold air. She pulls on her shirt. He reaches for his shorts.

"You use something, don't you?" he says. "Or take something? Like the pill or something?"

"Don't worry about it," she says.

He frowns, looking embarrassed.

"I should've asked earlier, but I figured you'd say something if I needed to—you know."

"I know, I know."

He groans and knocks his head against the wall.

"C'mon, how graphic do I have to get here? Does she or doesn't she?"

She laughs.

"She does, she does. Don't worry about it."

He kisses her on the forehead. It's the kind of kiss he could give his grandmother, and she likes it better than if he'd made a dive for the breast. It's sweet. Neither of them belongs here, and he's enough of a human being to know it.

"You know, this is when I really miss smoking," he says.

She's also missing something, but she's not sure what. She knows they'd have been smarter to talk about HIV tests than birth control and air conditioners, but that's not what she's missing, and it's too late to matter anyway. She sets the thought aside and tries to imagine she's smoking, drawing tobacco deep into her lungs, exhaling. He begins to tell her about his kids, a boy and a girl, seven and five. His ex doesn't want him to see them. She's remarried and thinks it would be better for everyone if he bowed out. But he worries about them. The way he and his ex fight—that sort of thing can damage kids. And the little one can't say her *R*s. It's kind of cute, really. You tell her to say *grrr* and she says *gaah*. But it's something else he worries about.

Cath has never seen Dave with his kids and didn't know he had any. She doesn't ask how far behind he is on his child support. She doesn't ask when he last saw them. She doesn't ask if they miss him. She wonders what it is about sex that makes men talk about their kids, their ex-wives, their cigarettes, their dead grandparents, everything they've ever lost in their lives, everything they either don't want or can't have back but whose loss they like to regret. One man, years ago, told her he'd been a boy soprano in the church choir.

The priest told him he had the voice of an angel. Then his voice changed. She can't remember his name, but she remembers the bar they'd been drinking in, and that no one bothered to card her. She remembers that when he told her this they were in the front seat of his car, and she remembers that he'd just raped her.

Dave is talking about his ex-wife. Cath thinks about red choir robes and the cigarette butts they stubbed out in the ashtray at the bar. She closes her eyes and focuses on the list upstairs, folded under the Swedish ivy. She looks forward to the things she'll miss: the smell of men's aftershave, the thickness of their wrists, the color of the snowbanks when she leaves the garage before dawn on a winter morning, the dispatcher begging for drivers to call in. She'll miss belonging to a secret elite that owns nothing and controls nothing but knows every bar, every supermarket, every business that's gone belly-up, everything that moves down a city street, and how to pry a living from all of it. She'll miss the lies drivers tell each other and the woman she picked up once near the detox, wearing a hospital robe and paper slippers, one eye purple and swollen almost shut. She lived above a florist and paid Cath in coins she shook out of a poodle bank. She'll miss Dave, with his children and his air conditioner, his jockey shorts and appendix scar. He's receding into the past already, the last man she ever slept with. They'll put their clothes on, watch television, and then she'll leave. The door will close behind her, and he'll be nothing but the memory of a voice, telling her how sweet it is to leave a life behind, and how much you miss it.

The Rules

Cath's leaning against the wall of a vegetarian restaurant listening to a woman with green hair read poetry. As far as Cath knows, she's alone in this room with thirty-six lesbians. The number's accurate—she knows this because she counted—but she can't say for a fact that they're all lesbians. What she can say is that she saw a poster for the event, and the poster billed it as a lesbian poetry reading.

Still, even if not everyone's a lesbian, two women are necking at a corner table, and it's fair to assume that they are. All right, they're not exactly necking, they're touching, but Cath's never seen so little happen so intensely. One has a hand on the other one's neck, which is long and thin and leads to a headful of hair that's no longer than Cath's thumb is wide. In fact, they both have buzz cuts, and they're dressed alike: white tee shirts, jeans, men's satin-backed vests, one black, one gray. They're gorgeous the way young boys are sometimes gorgeous, just before their hormones kick in and they thicken out and grow beards.

The one in the gray vest moves her hand up the other woman's neck, following its curve to the bristle-cut hair, and the woman in the black vest arches her neck forward, opening a broader field for her friend to touch. Cath imagines coasting her own palm over the blunt ends of that hair. She clenches her fists to keep the nerve endings occupied.

The green-haired poet's still standing in the open patch of floor that they're using for a stage, and she thanks the audience for being there. Everyone claps. Cath hasn't heard a word. At the corner table, the two women pound their hands together and whistle as if they'd had nothing but poetry on their minds this whole time.

The next reader wanders into the stage area and shuffles her papers. She has an edgeless quality and wears long, loose clothes. Cath turns away from the couple in the corner to focus on her, but all she absorbs are isolated words: women, blood, moon, goddess, earth. The woman doesn't say what goddess—it must be too obvious to need saying. The word *goddess* always struck Cath as a diminutive—a lesser form of god, the way priestess is a lesser form of priest or poetess a lesser form of poet. She can't see the point of embracing words like that.

The women in the corner are touching again. The one in the black vest has her head on the other one's shoulder, and the one in the gray turns to kiss the top of her close-mown hair. The poet reaches the end of a page and rustles it to the back of her sheaf. She has a handful of pages left. Blood, moon, tree, goddess, earth.

The third reader's good—Cath hears just enough to know this, but she's still not concentrating. She's taking a clothing inventory.

The most visible style, maybe because it's what Cath

expected lesbians to look like, is modified motorcycle. In fact, less than half a dozen of the women are dressed this way, and none of them are actually wearing leather. It has more to do with the way they hold themselves than with their clothes.

A larger group has the boy-girl look of the couple in the corner, although most of them have hair. They're feminine in a way Cath's never thought people could be feminine. She's pretty sure she couldn't pull this off herself—she'd look like her brother did at fifteen, with neither a boy's charm or a man's sureness—but it's a look she could live with if she had the chance.

And then there's a group Cath wouldn't be able to pick out if she saw them on the street. They're the most varied. One's actually wearing a skirt, ankle length and full of color. The only thing that marks them as not straight is something direct and unapologetic about their faces. She could live with this too.

More to the point, her parents could live with it.

Only the one woman has green hair. She doesn't fit any category.

During the intermission, Cath buys a cup of coffee and sips it, leaning against the wall and letting her eyes go out of focus so she won't look like she's expecting anything. She could introduce herself to someone if she wanted to. She could drop into an empty chair, look around the table, and say, "Hi, I'm Cath Rahven, and I don't know anyone here. Do you mind if I join you?" She could tap someone on the shoulder and ask if she actually believes in this goddess, and if so, which one it is. She could ask if believing is a requirement. She could ask if someone runs classes to teach newcomers the rules, the secret handshakes, the blood sacrifices. She swallows the last of her coffee and carries the cup to a cart where people are piling their dirty dishes. Her shoulder brushes someone else's, and she apologizes. The woman turns to her. She has small features, large eyes, a lavender satin necktie. Cath says again that she's sorry.

"Nothing happened," the woman says.

Cath nods several times as if she agrees. She has no idea what it means, but one of the rules is hidden inside it somewhere. If it made any sense at all to her, she'd be thrilled.

Becoming a Frog

Time passes. It's October, and Cath still hasn't slept with anyone. She feels like the frog prince in the fairy tale, only in this version he starts out human, and as soon as he kisses the maiden he turns into a frog. And, of course, he isn't a he.

Cath hasn't kissed the maiden yet, but she's leaning forward, eyes closed, lips puckered, trying to decide whether for one kiss it's worth spending her life as an amphibian.

It must be, because she can't keep her mind on anything else. She sees lesbians everywhere: in the supermarket, in passing cars, in her classes. She's gained second sight. She had no idea there were so many, and with each one she sees she imagines the touch of a hand, the softness of a cheek, the full-blown double dive onto the mattress.

What she can't imagine is what comes before that: how two women go from vertical and dressed to horizontal and panting.

The only lesbian she actually knows is Cynthia, and she knows her vertically. They have lunch together after their Social Work Problems class. Cath knows for a fact that Cynthia's a lesbian because twice she's mentioned her ex and called the person *she,* and the word raced along Cath's nerves like lightning hitting close enough to fry the wires—which is to say she acted as if it were nothing unusual.

Today Cynthia does it again. She says her ex called last night and told her she's moving to San Francisco in two weeks.

They're sitting in the student union coffee shop, each with a cup of university coffee and a sandwich from home. Cath wraps the twistie from her sandwich bag around the tip of one finger and then unwraps it.

"I wish I knew how I felt about it," Cynthia says. "I mean, once she goes it'll be all the way over, which is good because it's over anyway, if you see what I'm saying."

Cath sees. Cynthia sounds upbeat about it all. She has a cheerleader kind of energy that makes her upbeat about everything—fires, floods, and finals; plagues of locust.

"The thing is, I'm not really ready for it to be over. You know how that works, don't you?"

Cath doesn't, but she nods anyway.

"I should let go of her. I know that."

Cynthia pokes a finger into the bread of her sandwich, leaving a row of sinkholes along the edge.

"I think I must be depressed."

She says this brightly, smiling, then looks down and pokes another sinkhole in her sandwich. She takes a bite and holds the sandwich up to draw Cath's attention to it until she can swallow.

"I bought half a pound of salami on Sunday and I don't really like salami. *She* likes salami."

Cynthia smiles radiantly, and Cath does her best to smile back. She flattens the twistie against the tabletop.

"I noticed a couple of times that you mentioned *her*—"

This isn't what she meant to say, and it doesn't quite make sense at this point in the conversation. Cath's fingers run the length of the twistie, trying to iron it back into the shape it had before she wrapped it around the bag this morning.

"I mean, I noticed you said *she*, and I wondered if it's hard to just talk about that—"

This isn't what she meant to say either, and she shakes her head to fill out the end of the sentence.

"What, to straight people?"

"I don't know. I guess."

"You seemed like you were okay with it."

"I went to a lesbian poetry reading once."

Cath feels the blood rush to her face. She waits for Cynthia to laugh. Instead she says, "Was it any good?"

Cath has no idea, so she tells Cynthia she wondered what this goddess was that the one reader was going on about.

This time Cynthia does laugh.

"You can't take all that stuff too seriously. People get a little crazy with it, like they have to reinvent the whole world and make everything female. I don't know. The way I look at it, we're not all that different from straight people. When you come right down to it, it's only sex."

Cath's head swivels right, then left. On one side is a woman in blond braids, her head bent low over a textbook. Across the aisle on the other side is a group of corn-fed boys from the outer suburbs—snowmobile types. They don't care if it's only sex, or if it's also about politics or religion or, god forbid, feminism—they don't like it. Or they wouldn't if they knew about it. Cath leans forward, boring a tunnel under the noise so she and Cynthia can talk privately within it.

"And low-risk sex at that," Cynthia says. Her voice is half a gram too loud, and Cath winces. "Lesbians have the lowest venereal-disease rate of any category of people in the country."

Cath lifts her hands helplessly from the table. She wonders about the Amish—what's their venereal-disease rate? She wonders abstractly how Cynthia's defining her categories, although she doesn't much care.

Cynthia's voice drops down to a private level.

"Have you ever slept with a woman?"

Cath shakes her head.

"You ever think about it?"

Cath nods.

"Don't take this wrong or anything, but I think I could get interested in you."

Cath nods again. She doesn't know if she could get interested in Cynthia or not—she may be the only lesbian in North Port Cath hasn't imagined herself with.

A bit too late for it to be graceful, Cath says, "I'd be willing to try."

Cynthia laughs.

"Well, that's flattering."

"I didn't mean it like that."

Cynthia keeps laughing. She has small, even teeth

and a small nose. Her face is energetic and vivid. This isn't attraction yet, but if it had a chance, it might be.

Behind Cath, at the food counter, someone drops a tray of dishes. The boys across the aisle cheer. Cath turns but can't see anything. She turns back to Cynthia.

"So if we really are interested, what do we do?"

"We could go to a movie, go out for a drink—you know, have a date. Depends what you want to do."

Nothing this ordinary had occurred to Cath, and she can't tell if she's relieved or disappointed.

They end up on Friday night in a bar. It's not the one where Cath drove the bartender to work; it's one she never heard of. Except that the people in it are all women, it's like any other bar—smoke, alcohol, a juke box, a pool table.

Cynthia says she's sorry, she thought there'd be dancing.

"This is fine."

"Maybe it's better without it anyway."

"Maybe."

"It's okay, you know. We're just like anybody else."

"I know. I'm fine."

Cynthia's eyes drift toward the bar, and Cath's follow. The bartender's a solid woman in her thirties, the kind of lesbian Cath wouldn't have spotted until a few months ago, although she can't imagine anymore how she managed not to see it.

"The important thing is that you don't owe me anything," Cynthia says. "I mean, you shouldn't do anything you don't want to."

This is thoughtful, but Cath can't see how she's

supposed to know what she wants to do until it's too late to matter. She stretches a hand across the table and takes Cynthia's hand, which turns upward toward hers and unfolds inside it. Their fingers lace, unlace, and roll across each other, turning of their own accord, not quite under the direction of either of them. It's a form of dancing, only sexier and more private.

Some minutes later, Cynthia pulls Cath's hand to her lips, and a long time after that she says they could go to her place if Cath wants to, but one of her roommates is home tonight.

They go to Cath's apartment instead. Cath pulls the shades and stands in the middle of the room looking for some other way to barricade them from the world. She hangs their jackets up and shoves her hands in her pockets.

"You want some coffee or something?"

"Not unless you do."

They're standing about the same distance from each other as two opponents in karate before they bow and begin to spar.

"So," Cath says.

Cynthia stretches an arm out, and Cath walks into the space between them. She's as rigid as the floorboards under her feet, and she wishes she had some beer in the kitchen, or some wine. She wishes she'd had enough drinks at the bar to turn her mind to liquid. Cynthia puts her arms around Cath, and Cath looks over her head at the wall. At the bed, actually, which is shoved tight against the wall. She's never been hugged by anyone shorter than herself, and it's lonely—she wants eyes up where hers are. She puts her hands on Cynthia's shoulders.

"We don't have to do anything if you don't want to."

Cath shakes her head. This feels like all she's been doing with Cynthia—nodding her head, shaking it. She wants to make love with Cynthia, but she wants it the way she might want to jump off a high board: This first time, she'll have to force her feet to step out into the emptiness. She slides one hand lower on Cynthia's back, and then the other one. For a few seconds she moves them mechanically—the human body has a limited number of variations, and touching the back of a woman is not that different from touching a man's. After that, something else takes over, and Cynthia's back isn't at all like a man's. Then she stops thinking about it and simply touches.

She wakes up in the dark. Judging by the traffic outside, it's late night, not early morning. She lies on her back wondering who saw them come in, and who saw Cynthia not leave. Cath's apartment is in an old house, five apartments in all. The landlord lives next door. She knows most of the tenants well enough at least to say hello to, and she's no longer like any of them. Cynthia's wrong about that. Cath's stepped outside the circle of *us* and become one of *them*. Beside her, Cynthia lies curled on her side, breathing softly. Cath's never felt this alone in her life.

The next morning Cath drives Cynthia home and goes to work. The morning supervisor hands her the key to her cab. The dispatcher gives her a package run that goes out into the suburbs. No one notices a change.

They treat her the way they always have. This is either very natural or very odd.

After work Cath goes home, showers, and drives to Cynthia's. They call out for pizza and wait for her room-mates to leave.

They spend Sunday night at Cath's.

Monday evening Cynthia spends with her ex, help-ing her sort through things and pack. Cath catches up on homework and spends the rest of the evening writ-ing. She makes a few notes for the mystery she still hasn't started. In its current form, it's about the mur-der of a cab driver and the ambitions of his ex-wife, who's a radio talk-show host and running for mayor. It's just occurred to her that the police would try to trace the dead man's movements by the addresses on his trip sheet, but he'd faked them that day to cover the miles he took off the meter stealing a package run — something drivers do to keep from giving the company its percent of the fare.

Cath doesn't open the journal tonight. She doesn't want to write about Cynthia, and she doesn't want to put out the energy it would take to find some other topic in the world. Instead she works on a story about her father, which she started a few weeks ago. It's about how he played trumpet in a jazz band before she was born, and how she never once heard him play — not so much as a scale. It's about what a perfectionist he is, as if order were a substitute for the music he gave up. Writing it ties her throat in a knot, but she can't tell yet if the story's any good.

She adds a page about the bread truck he drove,

and the baked goods be brought home in the afternoon. She has no trouble telling the difference between jazz and pineapple sweet rolls, but she writes as if she did. She damn near convinces herself.

On Tuesday night, Cynthia stops by, wanting to talk about her ex, who she's calling by name suddenly: Karin, pronounced *Kah*-rin. *Kah*-rin'll be packing all week, sorting through everything she's ever owned, deciding what to keep, what to throw out, what to give away, and who to give it to. These are important decisions. Every object she owns is priceless. Even the toilet brush is in good taste. Last night, *Kah*-rin gave Cynthia a table that had been her mother's. It's a beautiful piece of furniture — dark, old, with carved feet. Cynthia's thrilled that *Kah*-rin wants her to have it. She'll have to borrow her roommate's pickup to move it.

Cath's imagined herself into Cynthia's house already. A roommate moves out, a room opens up. Everything that doesn't fit at Cynthia's, Cath stores in her parents' basement. Cath's apartment is an efficiency. She doesn't own much. But this table of *Kah*-rin's upsets the balance. It's like a seed from some strawberry jam that gets caught between two teeth, moving all the others over a fraction of a millimeter and throwing her whole mouth out of balance.

That night, Cynthia goes home to sleep. Cath works late the next day and spends the evening at the library. She doesn't see Cynthia until Thursday, in class. They meet in the hallway afterward and walk downstairs without either of them saying anything. At the front door, Cynthia says, "I need to talk to you," but she doesn't go ahead and talk. They push through the doors into the fall air. It's sharp, sunny, perfect. The sidewalks swarm with students—the U's ten-minute rush hour between classes. They turn toward the student union. A man with a white cane taps his way toward them, and the crowd parts self-consciously—the Red Sea scrambling aside for the Israelites, muttering, *Oh, excuse me, I didn't know I was in your way.* Cath moves a little farther onto the grass than she needs to. When she steps back onto the sidewalk, Cynthia says she's sorry but she doesn't think she can do it, she's just not ready for anything this serious.

Cath walks with her hands in her pockets. She wants to ask how serious Cynthia thinks they are. Whatever this is between them, it's not love. Too much of herself is standing back, keeping a list of weaknesses, bad habits, incompatibilities. They could go on if they wanted to, or they could turn in opposite directions and never see each other again. Either one would be fine. Instead, they buy coffee and find a table, because this is what they've always done.

"I shouldn't have gotten into anything this quickly is all. It's nothing to do with you."

"It's okay. I know what it's like."

"You're not hurt?"

"I'll be okay."

"I'd like us to stay friends."

Cath says she'd like that. Cynthia's face lights up—her cheerleader smile. Everything's settled. A minute later she's talking about her roommates. One of them's become a vegetarian and wants the whole house to stop eating meat.

Cath calculates the number of sandwiches that stand between them and the end of the term.

"What does she care what the rest of you eat?"

Cynthia shrugs.

"I don't know. She says it's a question of principle."

She doesn't seem to agree with this or to disagree. She looks bright, normal, and completely untouched by the oddities of the world.

Half the Risks

You don't choose your company when you drive cab. People open the doors, they sit down, and then there they are, just as if they were sitting in your living room. And so on the passenger side of Cath's front seat is a driver named van Dee, a frowsy blond who's clutching a cup of coffee like it's god's last remedy for a hangover. If Cath had been studying when he opened the door, she could have gotten rid of him, but she hadn't worked up the energy yet. She's taking a math class this quarter, Algebra for Idiots, a required course she should have taken as a freshman, and it's hard to make herself open the book.

Behind van Dee, a driver named Sam takes up half the back seat without having to sprawl. Sam's massive and in his fifties, and if all his stories are true he's been driving cab since before he was born.

Behind Cath, on the slice of seat that Sam leaves open, Frankie's wedged himself in. Frankie's the only one of the three that Cath wholeheartedly likes. He's been driving part-time for years. He's skinny, graceful, and—it occurs to her now with the force of revelation—almost surely gay. He's also a musician; he performs an improbable kind of Afro-New Agey music, mostly in coffee houses. Cath went to hear him once and was disappointed, but he plays the thumb piano for her in the cab once in a while, and each time he does she decides to go hear him again because she must have missed something last time.

The day's clear and unseasonably warm for two weeks into November, which means business is slow. They've been here a while, waiting for the doorman at the Ryland Inn to set a suitcase on the sidewalk, raise the braid-trimmed sleeve of his uniform, and whistle. They'd all make better money working the radio, picking people up at bars and doctors' offices, but they're gambling on airport runs, gambling that no one will walk up off the street and want to ride two-and-a-half lousy miles to wherever they live. By now they can't afford to give up on the stand any more than they can afford to stay on it.

Sam and Frankie have been talking about a driver who was fired for keeping his cab out for sixteen hours while he played cards at the airport. Frankie says the man's taking his case to the union, claiming he had stomach flu and couldn't make it back to the garage.

"Hey, they'll never prove it isn't true," Cath says. She's sitting sideways behind the wheel with her back against the door, leaving it up to van Dee to let her know if the doorman shows.

"Never prove it is, either," van Dee mumbles.

Cath starts to say something angry—she doesn't know what yet—but Sam cuts her off.

"Any of you ever hear about Paul Caffler?"

"Used to know a Caffler drove for Yellow," van Dee says. "Big guy, one ear that stuck out at a funny angle."

"Day driver?"

"Mostly."

"I remember him. Different guy. No relation. Paul Caffler was a night driver, never worked for Yellow in his life. Before your time, I think, all of you. Quiet sort, the kind of guy you wouldn't get to know unless you made a point of it. If he pulled up behind us here, he wouldn't come looking for company, he'd just pull out his newspaper and start reading. He had a thing about newspapers. Read anything he could get his hands on — Philadelphia, Chicago, San Diego. Anything. You got in his cab to talk to him, that's all he'd talk about, newspapers. He could tell you the scores if you asked, but he didn't much care about them. It was the paper itself he was interested in. Had names for all the different kinds of type they used and everything.

"Well, one night at the end of his shift, he didn't bring the cab in. He wasn't the kind of guy to do that, so they were worried about him and the dispatcher starts trying to raise him. After a couple of hours they called him at home, thinking maybe he got disgusted or drunk or something and went to take a nap, but he didn't answer there either. There weren't all that many cabs left on the street by that time, but the dispatcher asked the ones who were left to keep an eye out for him. Finally they decided something must have happened, and they called the police. His last run was at a bingo hall, and they tried to trace him from there, but he'd just disappeared.

"For the next three days, there wasn't a driver on

the street who wasn't looking for that cab. I can't remember what he drove anymore — sixty-two, sixty-three, something like that — but you can believe I knew it at the time, and every cab I saw, I checked the number. Every group of drivers you'd walk up to, somebody was talking about what they thought happened to him, or they were talking about the time they got robbed, or the time they almost got robbed, or about the driver who got his throat cut the year before and lay there gurgling into the mike while the dispatcher called the cops and then had to sit around waiting to hear sirens while the guy lays there bleeding. I'll tell you what I thought was they'd pulled Caffler off under the Deele Street Bridge and pushed him and the cab both right on in. Every time I got near the river I'd look down and wonder what all was under the surface of that water.

"Well, on the fourth day, finally they get a call in the office. It's Caffler, and he says he's met the love of his life, the woman he picked up at the bingo hall. She won some money and wanted to take a cab to Wisconsin, and on the way they fell in love and decided to chuck everything. He says they're in Niagara Falls, and if anybody wants the cab they can come get it. He and this lady are going to have a honeymoon and get married."

All four of them laugh. Cath glances at the empty sidewalk in front of the Ryland Inn, then turns back to look at Sam.

"Now here's the moral," Sam says. "A couple of

years later, I see him driving for Suburban, and he's still reading his papers. I heard him and his wife split up, if they ever did get married."

"That's not a moral," Frankie says. "A moral has to do with right and wrong, good and bad. Lessons about how to live your life."

"A quiet guy like that, you never know," van Dee says, talking over Frankie. "I knew a guy once, cousin of a friend of mine, farmer out by where I grew up. Sit in the VFW, suck on a beer all night long, never say more than 'How ya doin'' and 'Night.' Not a mean drunk, just quiet. Five years ago he shoots his whole family—wife, two kids, and himself. Newspapers asked the neighbors about him, they said they didn't know him all that well. Quiet guy. Kept to himself. All your mass murderers, your serial killers—quiet guys."

He falls back into silence, staring into the coffee-stained walls of his cup.

"You ever hear why they split up?" Cath asks Sam.

"I can tell you why," van Dee says. He sounds the way a lot of men sound when they talk to women, as if he can explain everything that happens in the world and is sick to death of having to.

"How are you going to tell her that when you don't know yourself?" Frankie snaps. "You never knew the guy. You knew the other Caffler, the one who drove Yellow."

"I can tell her what happened because it's what always happens. They got married, that's what happened. They moved in together, and suddenly there she was, morning and night. Guy wants to read his paper, she wants to know, 'Honey, don't you love me?' He says, 'Sure I love you, but I want to read the paper right now.' Well, sooner or later it's over. Don't take me wrong," he says directly to Cath, "but once a man moves in with a woman, there's no room in his life for anything but the woman."

He turns to give Frankie a look like the arrangement's his fault.

"That's why I'm single."

"Oh, *please.*"

"You think you know something I don't? Hah?"

"If you'll quit your squabbling, I'll tell you what happened," Sam says. "It's simple. Love doesn't last forever. There's only one thing lasts forever, and that's cab driving. Here's a man takes his cab halfway across the country, walks away from it, and then he doesn't tell anyone for four days. Burns his bridges, right? Can't go back. And what happens? A couple of years later he's driving again. You see how it is? It once gets in your blood, you can't get away from it. How long have you been driving?" he asks Cath.

"Little over two years."

"There's no future in it, you know that, but if you quit this afternoon I'll tell you what'll happen. For a month or so you'll feel great. You'll see a cab on the street, and you'll look at the driver and think, What a chump. Then one day you'll be downtown, and you'll find yourself checking the cab stands, wondering how business is, wondering if there's anyone you want to say hello to. Or you'll be driving along and you'll see somebody wearing a suit and standing at the curb with his arm in the air, and you'll swerve. You will."

"Not me, Sam. I get my degree, I'm outta here. I knew of a real job, I'd be gone already."

"Ha. You'll look at him, you'll see money going into somebody else's pocket, which is the same thing as seeing it go down the drain. *Right* down the drain. You'll be making better money and taking half the risks doing something else, and you'll still want the fifteen bucks he's going to drop getting to the airport. This isn't what you'll remember, sitting on a stand with this bunch of no-loads, killing time, wondering how you're going scrape together enough money to make it worthwhile having gotten out of bed this morning. It'll be like this never happened, and you'll come back. You wait and see. Sooner or later, you'll come back."

Cath glances at the hotel door. She says, "Not me," and Sam laughs.

"That's what they all say. I said it myself one time, and look at me now."

Cath does look. She doesn't see anything that reminds her of herself, but she has the uneasy feeling she's missing something any stranger walking up off the street could see.

Women

Winter passes, along with most of the summer. Experience accumulates. Women accumulate. It begins to dawn on Cath that there's a pattern here.

Take Lee. Part of Lee's appeal is that she's not Cynthia. She has depth. When she's feeling rotten, she doesn't plaster a smile over it. But Lee and Cath get used to each other, and one day Cath notices that Lee feels rotten more often than she feels good. Cath begins to wish she would smile. Emotional dishonesty is an underrated virtue.

Or Andrea. Andrea isn't either Lee or Cynthia. She has an interesting mind. She's stable, reliable, energetic. It takes them a week to find out they're not really attracted to each other.

April's attraction is that she isn't Andrea or Lee or Cynthia. The list begins to sound like a children's song: She went out with April to get over Andi; she went out with Andi to get over Lee.

With Megan, it never goes beyond a movie and a cup of coffee. Cath begins to believe she has congenitally bad judgment—some birth trauma scrambled her wiring and left her attracted to all the people she doesn't belong with and none of the ones she does. She avoids dances, parties, organizations of single women.

This is no great loss. She doesn't have enough time to start with. And in every age, hundreds of thousands of people have led productive, satisfying lives without being part of a couple, even if off the top of her head Cath can't name any of them. In the back of her mind she accumulates notes for an essay: "In Defense of the Single Life." We begin our lives single, and most of us end them that way, but our culture—not to mention Cath's mother—tells us we're failures unless we're coupled. She keeps a list of what's good about being single: It makes us take friendships more seriously; it turns us toward a larger world instead of to one other person all the time; it makes us self-reliant. It's also lonely as hell, and every human being she knows except her seems to be involved with someone.

She has no idea how they manage this, or how she doesn't.

An Antidote to History

On the way home from her uncle's, Cath bikes face first into a yellow jacket, and the force of the wind slams it against the skin under her eye and holds it there. Even as her hand reaches up, her brain's telling her to turn her head and let the wind blow it off. She has time to know that this is a good idea, but her hand keeps on rising and sweeps the yellow jacket aside.

The sensation of being stung comes to her in the drawn-out fraction of a second that it takes the yellow jacket to blow away behind her. She has time to notice that the sting hurts, then to think that bees die when they sting and that as far as she knows yellow jackets do too. This means the yellow jacket made a worse decision than she did. She has time to wonder whether she'd have fallen if she'd turned her head, and to worry that her eye will swell up so much she won't be able to see.

She pulls to the curb. Three women are waiting for a bus at the corner, under the shade of an elm, and she has an impulse to ride up and ask them to look under her eye for the stinger. She doesn't expect them to find it, or to be able to pull it out if they do, but she wants them to talk to her — not to tell her it's all right, but that it's terrible, it must hurt a lot, she's very brave. In the back of her head is the half-formed thought that if one of them has kids she'll know what to do.

Cath spends the rest of the day alternately lying down with an ice pack draped over half her face and working on a paper for her Psychotherapeutic Theories class. The assignment is to consider some aspect of her family of origin's functioning in light of insight therapy's approach to individual psychology.

Cath's grateful for the assignment. It's the only reason she went to her uncle's: to see if he didn't have some insight hidden away that she could surprise out of him. She doesn't come from the kind of family that volunteers information — or the kind that asks questions, for that matter. Her ambush was a departure, a breaking of the rules.

She's trying to be rational and adult about the scraps of information she managed to shake loose; this means she's focusing on the family as a whole, using something her uncle told her — that her grandparents didn't like her mother. They thought she wasn't good enough for their boy, and they didn't like it that she came from Chicago. Cath never knew this before, but it fits. It makes sense of the formality, the distance she remembers between her parents and grandmother, and it makes a nice argument for her paper: Her parents were isolated from both extended families, by geography on one side and bad feelings on the other. Money was tight and babysitters were scarce. They couldn't get away for an evening to draw a deep breath. And they had to show everyone they'd been right about each other. It was the ideal recipe for making two perfectionists even fussier. It may even explain why Cath gets claustro-phobic in relationships.

The problem is that her mind keeps slipping aside and fastening on something else her uncle said: that Cath's wrong to think her mother didn't want a girl. She seemed happy about it and was more relaxed with Cath than she'd been with Charlie. Why wouldn't she want a girl? She already had a boy.

Cath should feel good about this, but instead she's filed it with her grievances. They already had a boy, so a girl was fine. Dessert after the meat and potatoes; an afterthought to the important work. Damn it, she's used to the idea that her mother wanted a boy. In an odd way, it's impersonal. And she's rolled it under her tongue for so many years that it's lost its rough edges.

But if her mother really did want a girl, then what disappointed her was the girl she got. Cath sucks on this thought all afternoon. She takes the ice pack out of the freezer. She puts the ice pack back in the freezer. When she blinks, her eyelid slides over an iced marble. A semicircle swells up under her eye, a bag of poison larger than the insect it came from. This is physically impossible, but she's not going to split hairs while the semicircle's pumping poison into the flesh around it.

Every time she goes to the refrigerator for the ice pack, she checks the mirror to see what's changed in her face. She checks again when she puts the ice pack back. She checks so often she loses track of what it looked like last time, but the semicircle stays constant, like either the first or the last trace of a black eye.

She sets aside the paper she's been working on and

starts one that focuses shamelessly on what a lousy deal she got in her family. She's not tracing pathology here — she doesn't stand a chance in the who-got-screwed-worst sweepstakes. This is nothing more exciting than garden-variety sexism, but she's on the edge of tears all the same. She never got the attention her brother got, or the leeway, or — why not say it? — the love. Her father was distant from both kids. A decent man, but tired all the time. Hell, he got up at four, why wouldn't he be tired? Cath's strongest connection with him was through the mysteries he read and passed on to her. Not a wordless connection, but the words didn't belong to either one of them.

Cath's mother favored Cath's brother. Always.

Shouldn't this be bad enough? Part of her thinks it should be; the other part tells her to pull her socks up and stop whining. She puts this part on hold and gives herself over to loss, to self-pity, to connecting who she is now and who she might have been with what it meant to be a girl in her family. Gradually the swelling expands downward from her eye toward her chin. She feels like she's had novocaine and it's almost worn off but this last little bit won't leave.

By the time she goes to work the next day, her eyelid's swollen and she can trace the motion of each separate blink.

"It was a yellow jacket," she tells the dispatcher before he can either ask or not ask. "In case you thought I went down to the bar and got someone to slug me."

The dispatcher this morning is Carl, who's never said anything more to Cath than he could help. He swallows the beginnings of his sentences, as if he has to pay by the word and doesn't want to waste money on her. She's never bothered to say much to him either, but if you want to circulate gossip in the garage, you tell it to the dispatcher.

"You leave here," Carl says, "buy some antihistamines. Take the swelling down before your second run."

"Antihistamines," she echoes.

"Son got stung couple of years ago. Worked."

Cath says she'll try it. He lifts her key off the board and hesitates before he slides it out of the cage to her.

"Want to keep that from getting so bad next time — roll-on antiperspirant. Right away."

He drops his voice to say this, as if he's talking about tampons or something, and he mimes rubbing antiperspirant under his eye. Cath wants to echo the word back to him the way she did antihistamines, but she manages to say "No kidding" instead.

"Works," he says. "Carry it in the car. Kid knows it's there, keeps 'im from getting scared."

Cath thanks him. She hadn't known Carl had a kid, or that he loved anyone enough to carry something embarrassing. She'd like to say more than thanks — she'd like to tell him she's touched — but it would embarrass them both.

The antihistamines do take the swelling down, but the cheek stays puffy. Between runs she pulls the rearview mirror toward her to check for changes. By noon her mouth's pushed down in the corner so she looks like she's had a stroke. She doesn't expect the passengers to comment, but other drivers—people who've seen her when the two sides of her face matched—don't seem to notice it either.

In the afternoon she drives a nurse to one of the hospitals. It's a short run, but Cath wedges in a *Reader's Digest* version of the yellow jacket story. She can't seem to help it. She asks if the swelling means she's allergic to bees.

"It's a histamine reaction," the woman tells her. "You might want to be careful for a while."

This doesn't answer the question, but it makes Cath feel better.

The next morning the eyelid's puffed up again. She takes more antihistamines. By the time she leaves for school, it doesn't look bad, but the cheek feels like someone else's. The only way she can tell it's hers is that it itches a little and she's the one wanting to scratch. If she starts scratching, though, it's going to itch a lot. She takes another pill. The itching goes away but the half circle stays under her eye like the shadow of a bruise.

She doesn't know any way to circulate gossip at the U. They'll have to think whatever they want.

She spends two hours in the library working on the second version of her paper: Her mother wanted a girl she could dress up and decorate. She wanted someone sweet and pretty and passive. When she ended up with Cath, she decided this was the raw material for the daughter she deserved.

It occurs to Cath that from any given set of facts she can spin half a dozen theories. This doesn't increase her confidence in any of them.

She makes a list of things her mother said to her at one time or another:

> "Don't sit like that, you're not a boy."
> "If you'd only *try*, Cathy. You're not bad looking."
> "I don't care what Charlie can do. You're not Charlie."

By the third entry, Cath has a new theory: She was defined more by what she wasn't than by what she was. She's not sure what this means, or if it means anything at all, but like everything else just now, it hurts her feelings, or gives her already hurt feelings a new focus. She rubs under her eye, and the stinger comes loose beneath her finger.

This is a good omen. Once the source of the poison's gone, she can get better. But by the time she sets her paper aside to go to class, the eyelid's swelling again, and she needs another pill.

The next morning the eyelid's bigger than ever and the place where she got stung is an indentation in a sea of puffy cheek — the opposite of an island. She takes a double dose of antihistamines and her mind presents her with a split-second image of the way her mother used to brush a hand over Charlie's head when they were little, not to tame or curl or straighten like she did with Cath, but for the pure pleasure of touching him, the way she might run her hand over velvet.

Cath lets herself feel this, which is what insight therapy says you need to do if you want to go beyond who you've been. She feels rotten, but not in any new way.

So this is how it works: You name the problem, you find the source and dig it out, but the swelling goes right on. If the puffiness in her face is a histamine reaction, then the body's way of protecting itself is doing as much damage as the sting it was protecting against. Maybe it's doing more damage. Nothing's simple. She already knew this, or she should have, but she never quite stops hoping. She wants an antidote to her entire history. She wants to swallow a pill and walk into the rest of her life cleansed of everything she hasn't given careful thought to and chosen. She reimagines her mother's hand on Charlie's head but this time has it give his hair a sharp yank. This is immature and untherapeutic. It solves nothing for anyone.

She feels a whole lot better.

Starting Badly

Sunday. Cath wakes up slowly, without the alarm clock drilling holes in her dream. She lies on her back and remembers dreaming about water, about crossing a river and kicking up drops of water so they caught the sun. Connected to this is a startling sense of freedom. If she could call the dream back, she'd stay in bed all day and direct it through her life, element by element — school, job, relationships, karate, writing, her family. Especially her family. By the time she woke up on Monday, she'd run as clear as the river.

She remembers now that the river ran over sand. It's amazing that all this can happen inside her head and then disappear in the beat of a bird's wings — that she can carry on a whole separate life and know next to nothing about it in this one.

She folds the covers back and crawls out into the world. Birth, she thinks.

Well, rebirth.

All right, one more ragged morning.

She hates mornings.

She makes extra coffee and promises herself an hour to drink it and reread a mystery she likes. For this she has to set the alarm or she'll lose the whole morning. The author can't wind up a plot to save his life, but it's set in Mexico City, and the place alone is rich enough that the plot barely matters. At least to her it doesn't. Her father didn't like the book.

The alarm punches holes in the book, pulling her back to North Port. She marks her page, washes her cup and the plate that held her toast, wipes invisible crumbs off the table to mark the transition from food to work, then sets her books out.

On the far corner of the table, a green balloon wearing her cab hat rests in an empty mug. If she were to turn it around, it would say SAMPLER DRUG STORES on the face, but when she reaches toward it all she does is tip it more securely against the wall and consider whether to find a magic marker and draw eyes and a mouth on it. Nothing in her world has the resonance of Mexico City. She can't imagine anyone voluntarily setting a novel in North Port, but it's the only city she knows. She's stuck with it.

In front of her on the table is her notebook of sketches for the mystery. The ex-wife—the radio talk-show host who's running for mayor—has developed into a flamboyant local personality. She'll say anything that comes into her head, on the air or off, especially if it's about sex. She gives the station manager night-mares, but her ratings are off the charts. She broadcast live once from a massage parlor, interviewing the girls, the owner, the only customer who'd talk to her. Another time, she had herself tattooed on the air: a rose on the left breast—not some stingy little tasteful thing, she told whoever was listening; we're filling the canvas here, and let me tell you about the size of the canvas —

Her ex-husband gets killed after he tries to talk her out of running for mayor. Cath hasn't figured out what he knows about her that she doesn't want him to make public, but it has to be something the statute of limitations doesn't run out on.

All of which is fine, but Cath won't believe a word of it till it's on paper. She feels like she's selling herself a used car and is trying to weasel out of a warranty. She's swearing that if anything goes wrong, the boys in the shop'll take care of it. Hey, what do we need with a bunch of papers — one clever lawyer can make it all worthless anyway. We're friends here.

She picks up her pen and writes, "It had been a bad year for cab robberies, but something went wrong with the one involving Lyle Sexton. Three hours after his shift should have ended, he was found with a bullet through his brain."

She draws a couple of tornado-like squiggles in the margin and makes a note a few lines after what she's just written. "From here, follow whoever finds him — cop, driver, neighborhood kid?" Then she sets the notebook aside. If this is no worse than the other openings she's written, it's also no better. She can't imagine her father getting as far as the second paragraph if this is the first one. She tells herself not to worry about it, she has to work her way through some fixed but still unknown number of bad openings before she finds the right one, and this is one more out of the way. She tells herself the boys in the shop'll fix it, and then that it's not time to panic yet — she's at the stage where all she has to do is let her mind play with the story, piling up ideas and setting them aside until she graduates. Her father doesn't have to see any of it until it's done. Then if he doesn't like it, at least that won't stop her from writing.

This is reasonable advice. She'd believe it if it applied to someone else's work. She remembers the river in her dream and wonders what divide she thought she'd crossed, since she's still on the wrong side of this one.

She opens her biology text and starts to underline.

The Evolution of Flying Squirrels

In the style of karate that Cath studies, they don't wear
padding when they spar. They approach each other
barefoot and empty handed, and they aim each blow a
paper's thickness from the surface of their opponent's
uniform. And so when the bony edge of Cath's foot
drives past Sensei's sleeve and into the space occupied
by his arm, there's nothing to keep her from feeling the
density of human bone, or the break she just made in
this particular bone.

In spite of which she doesn't quite understand
what's happened until Sensei gathers his left arm in his
right, cradling it across his stomach, and takes a step
backward. His face shows surprise more than pain.
She thinks he makes a sound, but she's not sure. Too
many things are happening at once. He takes a second
step away from her and Cath drops her arms. Her fingers relax until they're not forming fists anymore. The
morning sun pours in through the plate glass window,
a blinding white that comes from bouncing off snowbanks. Sensei's ghi—his uniform—is also white,
freshly washed, and his belt is so worn that the black
outer layer has frayed at the edges and shows the
white-cotton core. Sensei likes to say that if people
study karate long enough, they become white belts—

beginners — again. Cath's not sure why that's a good thing, but he makes it sound like it is.

Tentatively, she takes a step forward. Her mouth opens, and a little girl's voice says, "Sensei?"

Sensei's name is Leon Kaplan. He's in his fifties and has thick black hair with a sprinkling of gray. He's small and concentrated and fast. On the wall that separates the main room of the dojo from his office and the dressing rooms, he posts translations of Japanese haiku and beautifully drawn Japanese characters that no one there, including him, can read.

No one at the dojo calls Sensei anything but Sensei, which is Japanese for teacher. Literally, it means *born before* — not as in having led previous lives but as in older, wiser. Cath wonders sometimes about Sensei's life as Leon Kaplan — about whether he has one anymore, or whether having an entourage has eaten away at him until even in his dreams people call him Sensei and consider it an honor to go out for a beer with him.

Sensei lowers himself to the bench where students and visitors sit to take off their shoes. Going barefoot is part of the etiquette of the place — part of its Japaneseness. He's still cradling his arm across his stomach to keep from jarring it. Only a handful of students are left at this time of day, and they cluster in a semicircle around him, four men and two women, all brown or black belts, the same group that works out every Saturday morning after the formal classes end. It's shaken them to find out that Sensei's bones can break, and for a long moment all they do is stare. Then Ray, a black belt with white-blond hair and a long reach, jams shoes on his bare feet and says he'll bring his car around. Sensei nods. A blast of cold air sweeps in as Ray leaves, and their heads turn to follow him past the plate glass window toward the parking lot on Meeker. He's wearing only a cotton ghi and shoes—no jacket, no hat, no gloves—and he half trots and half minces on the icy sidewalk.

Sensei asks for his own shoes, and Cath bolts toward his office, where she finds a pair of low boots, one sock folded precisely into each heel. She kneels in front of Sensei and scrunches a sock down toward its toe, stretching the cloth to both sides as she pulls it up so her fingers won't touch his skin. Outside the window, a bus lumbers past. She unlaces Sensei's boots and fits them onto his feet, Prince Charming to his Cinderella, pushing with one palm against the heel, locking her jaw against what she expects to feel but doesn't: the grating of bone against bone, as if she'd broken his ankles too.

She stands. The other woman in the group, Laura, drapes a jacket around Sensei's shoulders. When Ray trots in from the street in a blast of cold air, Sensei rises to meet him.

And then they're gone. Cath moves away from the cluster of students and stands looking out the window. If she could disappear right now, everyone else would feel free to talk. And she'd be glad to disappear, but crossing the floor to the dressing room is beyond her. She brushes the sole of each foot clean against the opposite leg of her trousers, leaving a smudge on the cloth and a shower of grit on the floor.

Cath has studied with Sensei for five years now, and for the past two years she's been a brown belt. She's tested twice for black, but her sparring hasn't been confident enough. "It's as if you're afraid of your opponent," Sensei told her after the last test, and she nodded, not agreeing or disagreeing, just acknowledging what he said, although in a paralytic sort of way she is afraid. Her muscles move normally, but something inside shuts down. If it didn't, she'd run off the floor yelling, *Ma, he's trying to hit me.*

This morning, she asked Sensei to work with her on this.

"Sometimes," he told her, "if you want to change your karate, you have to change your personality."

"Sensei," she asked, "how do you do that?"

He laughed and said he had no idea—he'd hoped maybe she'd know.

"It would help if you trained more often."

"I'm in school," she said. "I work."

The pitch of her voice swore that the dog had eaten her homework.

Until he motioned her onto the floor after the last class, she wasn't sure whether he'd meant he'd work with her or that he couldn't be bothered.

Changing her personality isn't what drew Cath to karate. She wanted to know she could, well, break someone's arm if she had to. But now she wonders whether the process doesn't work in both directions: If having broken Sensei's arm changes her karate, will her personality also break open so she can rearrange the pieces?

Cath doesn't think of herself as someone who's afraid, but there are things that scare her: deep water, heights, walking on frozen lakes. Sparring. They're none of them crippling. If she has to go on living with them, she can. It's a kind of strength, knowing how to live with weakness. But if her personality's going to change, these are things she wouldn't miss.

By the time Cath reaches the dressing room, Laura's standing at the sink in her underwear, sponging under her arms with a wet paper towel. She looks at Cath in the mirror.

"Jesus, you really did it," she says.

Cath can't tell if she's congratulating her or scolding her. She drops onto a folding chair and rests her head in her hands.

"Hey," Laura says. "It's the risk we all take." She throws the towel into the trash, wets another, and sponges her face, shoulders, and neck. She faces Cath and rests her left foot against the opposite thigh to wipe the sole of her foot clean. Laura used to be a dancer, and everything she does is graceful. Her dancing is both the strength and the weakness of her karate. She picks up techniques easily. She can remember any sequence of moves. But she's trained her body to be weightless, and in karate you draw power from slamming your weight into the ground for a second and then releasing it. In spite of which, Laura's a black belt, while Cath is stalled out at brown.

"The thing is," Laura says, "you fought well."

"I didn't," Cath says, although she doesn't really know this. There's a tiny gap in her memory that begins just before her foot drove through Sensei's bone. She's not sure how her foot and his arm ended up occupying the same space at the same time. Maybe she closed her eyes; maybe her eyes were open but the pathways of her brain refused to record anything this unlikely. What she does know is that until her memory shut down, this fight was like all her others.

"It was a mistake," Cath says. "I didn't know his arm was there."

Laura cleans her other foot without bothering to answer. Cath unties her belt and opens the safety pin that holds her jacket shut.

"Besides, I was scared shitless."

She folds her jacket in half and lays it on the chair.

"That'll change," Laura says. She grins at Cath, then turns to lift her black-brown halo of hair a fraction of an inch farther from her head.

Only two students are left in the dojo, and they're sparring when Cath and Laura come out of the dressing room. They circle slowly, as if by breaking Sensei's bone Cath's wrapped them in invisible padding, muffling their movements. They don't break their rhythm, but Cath feels their eyes graze over her for split seconds—long enough to lose a match to any opponent who wasn't just as distracted. Cath's eyes graze over them as lightly as theirs do over her. She wonders if her standing in the dojo has gone up or down. She's not comfortable with either possibility.

Standing isn't a word Sensei's students use, but even so it orders their lives. They circle around him like the nephews of a childless king, trying to stand out in the crowd. They consider it an honor to teach for him, an honor to lead a class through its warm-up exercises, an honor to help demonstrate a technique.

The problem is, there's no predicting where his glance will land—on the best student, on the closest one, on the one who's been thinking about quitting. These things are governed by the laws of chance, or chaos, or economics. No given action has a known outcome.

Cath tries not to care about Sensei's praise, or his lack of praise, but even so she always knows where he is in a room. If he nods his approval, it satisfies a hunger she's known for so long she barely has words for it. Or she does have words, but she doesn't like them. She wants him to say she's as good and strong and visible as her brother. Or more so.

Her brother, of course, is nowhere around. He's never studied karate, and he moved to Chicago two years ago. Sensei's never met him. This is ancient history. It's past time she let it go, but she hasn't, somehow, and knowing that is like being seven all over again— always younger, always smaller, always female and less important. Always not knowing something her brother does know, or not allowed to go someplace he can go.

Cath doesn't think about her brother much. Even before he moved, she only saw him on holidays, but she has a shirt that she took out of his suitcase when she was sixteen, the night before he moved out of their parents' house. It's blue flannel, and by now it's so soft it's almost translucent at the elbows. She has to double the cuffs back to keep them from hanging down past her fingers.

When she took it, she had no idea why she was doing it. All she knew was that it was his and that he wanted it. Now she thinks it was an attempt at magic — when she stole his shirt she was stealing his power, except of course that it didn't work. All she ended up with was a flannel shirt. Every so often she decides to return it, but she's never figured out what to say about why she has it. Besides, she likes the shirt, and some threadbare part of herself still believes in its power.

Cath and Laura walk to the parking lot together. The radio this morning predicted warmer weather, but Cath can't feel it. The air's dry and sharp. Laura asks if she has time for a cup of coffee.

"I think maybe I need to be alone for a while."

"You're not going to quit, are you?"

Cath says no, she's not going to quit, although in fact when she wrapped her ghi in its brown belt to take it home, she looked inside her locker to see if there was anything she'd feel bad about leaving. She saw a three-dollar hairbrush, a string of safety pins, a clean undershirt. The lock itself. She doesn't believe she's quitting — it was just a thought passing randomly through her head—but she can't see how she'll walk back in the door with everyone watching her.

They stop beside Laura's car, and Cath stoops to pick up a piece of broken glass and throw it onto a snow bank. Laura has her car door open.

"Maybe I'll take you up on that cup of coffee," Cath says.

She doesn't remember making a decision about this. She didn't know she was still thinking about it at all. But it sounds better than going home.

They drive separately. In order not to lose Laura, Cath has to drive the way retired men drive in big cars, slowing down before traffic lights in case they turn yellow, drifting around corners as if she were poling a barge. To keep herself busy, she flips switches on the dashboard and turns dials. The fan blows cold air and a shaving of ice up the windshield. On the radio two men start talking about evolution.

"What I've never understood," one of them says, "is how anything evolves into a bird. I mean, what do you do when you've only got half a wing."

The second man laughs comfortably. This is the community radio station, and the interviewer's less polished than whoever he's interviewing.

"So far as we know," the second man says, "no bird has ever evolved from the ground up. They start in the trees. If you set aside the fact that it's a mammal, you can think of the flying squirrel as a kind of intermediate stage. It starts in a tree and it coasts down. Birds began the same way."

Cath thinks about the flying squirrel. It doesn't answer the question of what you do with half a wing. She glances in the mirror for Laura's battered Renault. She's a quarter of a block behind, dragging like a weight Cath has to tow. Cath downshifts. They're barely topping twenty. On the radio, the interviewer's saying, "It's like we've got the life span of a mayfly, and evolution has our life span, you know? We live one day. Mate and die. And all this great stuff—squirrels evolving into birds, all these other changes—they happen too slow for us to see them."

Cath twists the volume dial to the left, cutting off whatever the expert can say to that. She shuts off the fan. In the silence, every bump in the street is sharper, as if Sensei were in the seat beside her, his mismatched bones jabbing into his muscles with every jolt.

The place Cath takes them to is called Lois's. It's a breakfast-all-day place—hash browns, eggs, white-bread sandwiches. Cath likes it because Lois makes her own pie. Cath and Laura walk in together, and Lois greets them by saying today's pies aren't ready yet, but she's got some chocolate left from yesterday. Cath looks at Laura to make sure this is okay.

They sit in a booth by the window. Cath's never spent time with Laura except in class, or with Sensei and a group of karate students. She has no idea what to say to her. She shrugs and tries to smile and is saved from having to follow this up by Lois bringing them coffee.

Lois is in her fifties and has permed hair and deep red lipstick.

"Where's your cab?" she asks.

"I'm off today."

"Must be nice."

Cath gives her the grin she expects: Yeah, sure, it's wonderful. When Lois turns away to get their pie, a second's panic rises from Cath's belly up to her throat. Laura leans forward, looking warm, concerned, and for no reason Cath understands, disturbing.

"So how're you doing?" she asks.

Cath stirs cream into her coffee and licks the spoon clean.

"I'll be all right. I'm fine." She shakes her head. "When I finish my pie, I'll go home and fall on my sword."

She expects Laura to laugh, but instead she leans forward even more intently.

"Let me tell you something about what happened back there." She nods in the wrong direction, but Cath understands that she means the dojo. Cath leans forward to meet her, then pulls back to let Lois set their pie down. Laura smiles her thanks and pushes hers aside. Her eyes lock onto Cath's again.

"You ever hear the saying, 'If you meet the Buddha on the road, kill him'?"

"I didn't kill anybody," Cath says. She's serious about this. It doesn't strike her as funny until she hears herself say it. "I only maimed him a little."

This time she does make Laura laugh, but she

doesn't pull back to her own side of the table or let her eyes drift away from Cath.

"You ever think about teaching?" Laura asks.

"Jesus no."

"Why not?"

"Because I don't want to be a buddha, and I don't want to be a sensei. I don't even like warming up a class."

"Why not?"

Cath shakes her head and stabs at her pie a couple of times.

"I'm just a background kind of person."

Laura laughs.

"Not anymore you're not."

Cath uses the tines of her fork to scrape patterns in the top of her pie.

"Would you mind if we talk about something else for a while?"

Laura nods her agreement, but Cath doesn't have a topic to start them on, and she mangles her pie until Laura takes pity on her and says Ray must think he's died and gone to heaven, sitting in the emergency room next to Sensei for the next who-knows-how-many hours.

Ray's a karate bum. According to what Cath's heard, he hasn't held a job since he got his green belt, and she repeats this now, hoping it's true. Laura says if she were his wife she'd have been out the door years ago.

Cath's met Ray's wife. She's a school counselor — thin, brittle, self-effacing. Cath says she'd have been out the door too, absolutely, there's no point in staying with a man like that.

When they leave the cafe, Laura stops outside the door and asks how to get back to the dojo. She's headed home but has to start from someplace she knows. Cath tries giving her a shorter route, but Laura waves her hands to block the information, saying it'll only confuse her, she's dyslexic behind the wheel of a car. She says this without apologizing, the way a person might say *I'm nearsighted* or *I have a bad ankle.* They face south so they're looking in the direction Laura will face when she climbs into her car. Cath acts out the turns with her arms, not trusting the words *left* or *right* to carry any meaning. Her eyes water from the cold and the sun. She crosses the street with Laura and sits in her own car until Laura backs up, pulls into the empty street, and turns right. Still Cath doesn't start her car. The sky's achingly blue, and the branches that curve against it are black. She thinks about following Laura back to the dojo and asking whoever's left to spar with her. She can't string together the words she'll use, but she knows what she wants: She wants to fight till she loses and balance is brought back to the universe. She doesn't want the shadow defeat you get from sparring; she wants to come away bruised and aching. This is new. It's not what she wanted, but it's new.

When she pulls away from the curb, Cath tries to drive without a direction in mind — she's read about people doing this when they're upset — but she knows the city too well. She can't forget which street leads to what; can't help thinking ahead to the next intersection and asking herself whether to turn there, and which way, and why. After a handful of random turns through residential streets, she heads for a through street and drives to Pascoe Park, where she kills the engine, leaves her sunglasses in the car, and follows a woman and a rangy black dog downhill into the park. Pascoe's a small park, built around a pond, and the path divides to circle it. The woman and dog turn right, and when Cath hesitates instead of following them, the woman unclips the leash from the dog's collar, letting it run ahead.

Cath watches them go, then plows straight ahead into the snow, her legs churning a rough path toward the edge of the pond. At the shore, she hesitates again. The wind's blown the snow into a drift against the pond's stone wall, and for about a yard it's too deep to walk through. This comes as a relief. As long as she was sitting in the car, she was sure she could reach the edge of the pond and keep on walking. But ice is made of water, which is not a solid. People fall through the ice and die every winter: snowmobilers who get drunk and roar over ice where it's been undermined by currents; idiots who drive their pickups across lakes either too early in the season or too late; dogs; unwary kids. Cath believes in the power of gravity, even at five below. She believes in her own vulnerability. She believes that all the threads of a personality are woven together, and that if you pull one of them, the others will shift their pattern around it. If she can walk on ice, she will be changed in some way she can't predict. She turns left, circling the pond through calf-deep snow. On the far side, the city keeps a skating rink cleared, and this strikes her as a safer place to walk. A handful of people are skating on it, and not one of them has fallen through since she's been watching. Not that it matters. If this had anything to do with logic, she'd have talked herself out of being afraid years ago.

She unzips her jacket at the collar and pushes her scarf aside, letting the cold air chill her neck. Under her jacket, she's beginning to sweat.

Beside the wooden walkway that leads from the park building to the skating rink, she stops and rests her hand on the rail, breathing hard. A man is skating backward with a child who can't be more than four, holding his hands out to her, arms stiff, keeping a space open for her to stumble into. The girl's cap is turquoise and red with a double tassel. Cath's eyes water, and she touches them with the thumb of her mitten. Instead of soaking in, the tears nestle into the weave and glisten like tiny jeweled Easter eggs. Her neck's cold, and she pulls the scarf across her throat and takes a step closer to the ice. She rubs her hand backward and forward on the railing. She thinks about flying squirrels. She has no trouble imagining the action of half a wing, but she can't imagine its use. She takes another step forward and stands at the edge of the ice, separated from it by the snowbank that circles the rink. She ducks under the rail to the walkway and sets both feet on the ice. The weave of her personality doesn't shift. She doesn't lift into the air and fly. But neither does the ice split open and swallow her. She lifts her hand off the rail and steps farther off shore. A speed skater whizzes close to her shoulder and curses her for standing still. At the far side of the rink, the four-year-old collapses her legs and giggles while her father struggles to hold her up. Cath steps back until her hand touches the rail and it's easier to breathe.

Cath turns out the light beside her bed, settles her head into the pillow, and feels Sensei's bone breaking against the edge of her foot. She rolls over and stares at the pale oblong of the window shade.

Think of something else. Think of nothing. She closes her eyes and counts each breath. Two. Three. She's breathing too quickly. Four. Relax the body and the mind will follow.

She's fighting, not with Sensei but with someone faceless and male. She steps forward, kicking side-thrust to the kneecap. This isn't sparring; they're trying to hurt each other. He slips to the side and lands a punch on her ribs. She turns toward him, not even pretending to defend herself, and offers her face.

She rolls over and rechoreographs the match, making herself fight harder, pushing the man back toward the wall. She can imagine hitting him, but it's like punching a marshmallow—it doesn't hurt him, and it doesn't satisfy her.

She rolls over. She counts her breaths. Three. Four. She hasn't been back to the dojo since she broke Sensei's arm. She's written about it some, but it's journal writing—pointless whiny stuff. She keeps trying to bring it to a resolution: The lesson is this, the lesson is that, only it doesn't matter because at night she keeps having this fight. Four. Or is it five? She starts from one again, reaches two, rolls over.

She feels the break in Sensei's arm.

If nothing else has happened, at least her karate's changed. She can tell that by the pictures that dance through her head. She may be hell-bent to get hurt, but she's not afraid of being hit, and even in her imagination she used to be. She's not sure it's an improvement, but she feels the change as surely as she feels the cold at the foot of the bed every time she rolls over. She's more sure of herself. She's solider. That's all to the good, only she hasn't forgiven herself for it yet, hasn't let go of whatever demon it is that wants her to pound herself back into submission.

She opens her eyes and asks herself what she expected. That a lifetime's habits would pack up and leave without a trace? The answer, of course, is yes — she wanted to be a different person. Why should that be so hard? This is America. She's pursuing happiness.

She rolls over and starts from one again.

Stepping into the Air

Dave fits a rifle to his shoulder and sights down it at a star the size of Cath's fingernail. From every direction, the midway pounds noise at him. The siren on one of the rides screams like a litter of baby cop cars yowling to be fed, and at the next booth a carny calls, "Three for a dollar, hey, a prize every time."

None of this breaks into the silence Dave's drawn around himself. His cheek lies against the rifle stock as softly as if it lay on a woman's breast.

Standing behind him and to one side, Cath sinks herself as far as she can into his trance. She feels the balance of the rifle and for a second touches the quiet center inside the noise. Then Dave lets loose a burst of shooting that makes her jump. She'd forgotten this would happen. She watches the BBs chew up the star like overamped pacmen, and when Dave pulls the target toward him, she's ready to admire his aim.

"Oh, close, man, close," the barker says. He's on Dave's other side, a skinny guy in a dark green tee shirt. "Just the one corner."

He picks up one of the rods of BBs that he uses to load the guns.

"Tell you what, give me two bucks and try it again."

"Sights are off," Dave says.

"Shouldn't be. Here, use this one."

He picks up the next rifle and loads it. Dave pulls two singles out of his wallet and presses his cheek to the stock.

Cath's felt this kind of perfect, empty balance a couple of times in karate, and watching Dave she wishes she'd made herself go back after breaking Sensei's arm. It doesn't occur to her that she could go back now. The rest of her life has poured into the space karate once filled, and she doesn't have time for it anymore. It's like when people quit smoking—they should have lots of money left over, but they never do somehow. Nature abhors a vacuum, and she's none too fond of a surplus either. Cath catches a glimpse of herself suddenly, standing behind Dave in the position of the admiring girlfriend or the woman waiting beside the stew pot for her man to bring home a haunch of brontosaurus.

Dave shoots and pulls the target toward him.

"Sights are off. I should've had that."

"Tell you what, you give me three dollars, pick any two guns you like."

"Sights are off on all your guns."

Dave turns to Cath.

"Damn sights are off. You can't hit anything if the sights are off."

"It's all right. I wasn't hungry anyway."

Dave gives her a blank look and starts them walking.

"I thought I'd win you one of those snakes. Give me a gun that's sighted in right, I'm a decent shot."

Cath turns back to look at the snakes hanging from

the ceiling of the booth—six feet of green- or purple-and-white plush. They're not just inedible, they're hideous.

"What'm I going to do with a snake? You win something, give it to Cheri."

"Cheri finds out I've been with you, she'll hand me my head."

They step over a bundle of electrical cables. A breeze flicks past and is gone by the time Cath thinks to lift the hair off her damp forehead.

"I made a major mistake when I first got together with her," Dave says. "You know how it is, those first couple of weeks when you can't tell the difference between sex and shooting your mouth off? Well, I told her about—you know, you and me that time. That it was something that just kind of happened. So now she thinks we're dying for another chance. Every time she comes over, I expect her to bring cardboard boxes and start packing my stuff. Get me out of your clutches."

Cath laughs. Going to bed with Dave got something out of the way for both of them, and they've been on good terms ever since. The problem is that Dave can't bring himself to tell Cheri how lousy he and Cath were together any more than she can bring herself to say it to him now.

"Dave, you go out with the wrong kind of woman," she says instead.

Dave stuffs his hands in his pockets and doesn't do anything to let her know he heard—or that he didn't. They're at the turning of the midway and the roller coaster's thundering over their heads.

"You know, it really frosts me what they do with those sights," he says, bending toward her to yell into her ear.

Cath says uh hunh. Half her mind is listening to him, the other half is snagged on the words *you go out with the wrong kind of women*. The barb on them cuts as sharply as if he'd said them to her, or she'd said them to herself.

It's none of her business who he goes out with anyway.

"I don't mind losing an honest game. I don't like it, but I don't go around whining that it's somebody else's fault. But something like that, sighting them in wrong, that really frosts me."

Cath says uh hunh. She wonders how he can tell that the sights are off, but it doesn't seem important enough to ask about. She has no reason to think they're not.

Dave walks with his eyes on the ground. He looks like a man's nothing on the midway without a prize to cart around, or for the woman with him to cart around. He nods at a booth with rings and Coke bottles.

"You want to try that?"

Cath peels a dollar off the roll she put in her front pocket before she left the house—the exact amount she's willing to blow here, measured out as precisely as the amount of time she can steal from studying. She doesn't do this because she wants to play the damn game or because she expects to win it but to keep him from thinking he should fish money out of his pocket for her. She throws a couple of rings.

Dave stretches his arm over the barrier and makes a sideways motion with his wrist.

"Like this. Gently."

The motion he's showing her is no different than what she's been doing, or if it is she can't see the difference.

"No one wins this," she says.

"Why'd you give 'em your money, then?"

"You keep hoping. It looks so simple."

She has four rings left and hands him two. They fall where hers did, between the necks of the bottles.

"It's like the lottery. You know you won't get it, but you think, what the hell, if you did you'd really have something."

When they finally leave the midway, Dave's collected an inflated plastic crayon and a small stuffed dinosaur. He looks happier. They pass booths selling corn dogs, deep-fried cheese curds, mini-donuts. Cath breathes in the airborne grease and feels her shorts get tighter around the waist.

"So what's Cheri really like?" she asks.

Dave shrugs.

"You've met her."

Cath has met her, twice, for seconds at a stretch. She's pretty, she's carefully put together, and if there's more to her than that, Cath hasn't seen it. Except for Cath, who he didn't exactly pick, Dave chooses women for their looks and then wonders why things go wrong between them.

"But what's she *like*. How're you getting along?"

She has an impulse to keep adding questions until

she figures out what she wants to know and why it should matter.

"We're okay. We're great."

He grins to show her how great they are. Cath gives up on the question and stops to buy a bag of cookies that are the size of bottle caps. She forgets about Cheri until half a block later, when he says, "Tell you the truth, I'm not sure how we're doing. We've hit that stage —"

Cath waits. They pass the gate where they came in and Dave steers left, between the animal barns — swine on the left, cattle on the right. On a bench, an elderly couple sits watching the show pass by: bikers with tattoos the size of murals, clusters of girls in blouses that leave their midriffs bare, parents pushing their children in strollers or hauling them along by the arm or pulling wagons where they sit like the kings of very small islands.

"What stage?" Cath says finally.

"The stage where what we've got isn't good enough anymore."

He reaches into the cookie bag that Cath's holding open between them.

"She doesn't like the way I eat," he says.

Cath turns to see how he is eating, but the cookie's gone already. She's split a pizza with him a couple of times when they watched TV together, but she never paid attention to how he ate it. He didn't do anything bad enough to draw her attention — didn't throw his food, didn't end up wearing it.

A minute later, he says, "It's little stuff, you know?

My shoes, my car, my tone of voice, that kind of thing. I don't know. You think it's something I'm doing, or are all women like that?"

"Hey, what do I know?"

It's on the tip of her tongue to tell him again that he goes out with the wrong kind of women, but she's afraid he'll have to hear her this time and will ask what she means. If she thought he knew the answer, she'd ask what his tone of voice was and why Cheri didn't like it. She thinks how lucky they were to be lousy in bed together. She nibbles the outer edge off a cookie so that all she has left is the dime-sized center.

"You know what it is, we've hit the stage where she wants to change me. I told her when we met, I wasn't marriage material, I tried that once, and I'm not cut out for it, but I don't think she believed me."

Cath nods. Dave may not be marriage material, but he's still lonely. What's he doing here with her if not filling time with someone who'll keep her distance? That's the problem with the lone-cowboy routine—it looks better from the outside than it does when you're walking around in it.

Another breeze starts up and dies. All day a storm's been hanging over the city, and even though the forecast is for heavy air all week, each breeze makes her think that now, finally, the sky's ready to break open and let a cold front blow through.

At the bungee jump, they stop to watch. The outfit running it wants fifty dollars for a chance to hurl yourself at the earth and live through it, and no one's taking them up on the offer right now. A crowd's clustered around, though, waiting for someone to show up with the right combination of money and death wish.

"You ever think about doing that?" Dave asks.

"Waste of money."

"Forget the money. I'm talking about the jumping. Would you do it?"

Cath doesn't have to think about this. No corner of her being wants to step off a platform into the air and hope an oversized rubber band will yank her back up just before she splatters all over the ground.

"I don't stay up nights looking for a way to do it, no. Do you?"

"I could do it, yeah. I went sky diving with a buddy at work, and there's this moment when you're falling, before the parachute opens, where there's nothing but you and the wind and the ground coming up at you, and you know if you can do that you can do anything. I even dream about it sometimes—jumping, flying, hang gliding. Any of that kind of thing."

Cath dreams about flying sometimes, but she skims close over the ground, following hallways and sidewalks, amazed that she can do this much. Even in her dreams, she's either a coward or a realist.

There's a flurry of activity around the crane and the platform rises with two men on it. When it stops, one of them steps into an open space in the railing and stands with his back to the crowd. He freezes there so long that his fear radiates three stories down to the people on the ground. Maybe it's four stories, or five. There's nothing to measure it against. After ten or twelve feet, it doesn't matter anyway. The moment stretches out painfully. Cath watches and thinks about Dave crawling out of bed every weekday morning for the rest of his life, making a pot of coffee, and going to work, all the time wishing he were in midair, falling toward the earth. It all seems sad and pointless. She thinks about Dave's kids, about Dave and his ex-wife, about Dave and Cheri, about Dave and her, about Dave and anyone — about Dave thinking that if he can jump out of a plane he can do anything, but having a real relationship isn't on the list of things he wants to do. She thinks about how obvious this gap in his life is to her and how little good it would do to tell him about it.

"If you had to tell me one thing I'm doing wrong with my life that I don't know about, what would it be?" she asks him.

He glances at her, then looks back at the jumper, who's still frozen above the crowd. He doesn't want to miss the moment the man steps off the platform, and he doesn't want to miss his fear, because without fear the jump's worthless.

"I don't know. You take it all too seriously. You worry too much."

"Don't you?"

"You didn't ask about me."

Cath accepts this, but as revelations go, it's not much. It's not a revelation at all. Or if it is, it's too profound for her to absorb yet.

The jumper steps away from the opening, talks to the other man on the platform, then steps back. Whatever revelation the other man handed him, it was enough. He balances in the opening for a few more seconds, sets a foot out into space, and falls. The bungee stretches, pulls him up almost even with the platform, and lets him drop again. He whoops. When his rebounds get small enough, the platform sinks toward the ground, and someone catches him and sets him upright. He holds both hands above his head like a winning boxer. The crowd cheers. He's proved that he can do anything he wants to. Now he's free to sink back into his life, his job, his loneliness, and his relationships, leaving everything exactly the way it's been all along.

Change

"Let me show you something," Cath says.

She slams the door of her cab and comes around to the passenger side. The man she's talking to slams his own door, stranding the woman he's with in the back seat.

"See that?"

Cath points to the lettering on his door.

"Right there. Driver does not carry more than twenty dollars in change."

The passenger doesn't look at the door. He stands on the leaf-blown sidewalk, glaring at Cath, eight inches taller than she is and close enough to connect if he decides to swing.

"I'm going to say this one more time." He separates each phrase from the next to make sure she gets it. "I'm going in the bar, I'm going to get change, and I'm going to pay you two dollars and sixty-five cents because that's what the meter said when we got here. You want any more than that, too fuckin' bad."

Cath runs her hands through her hair and says, "Son of a bitch." She takes a deep breath. "Look, you need to get change, fine, go get change, but it's not my problem. The meter keeps running."

She's been through this already, before they got out of the cab, but she can't think of anything new to say. To make up for that, she turns up the volume, and when the passenger answers, he does the same. The arguments have all been made, and now they'll settle it by finding out who can shout the loudest. In some cool, self-enclosed part of her brain, she knows this is crazy, but the rest of her brain, along with the full weight of nerve and muscle and the internalized collective of every cab driver she's ever known — none of these are listening. They're worried she'll let this bastard take advantage of her. She says "Son of a bitch" again.

"You call me that one more time, I'll push your teeth down your throat."

"I'm not calling you fuckin' anything."

Cath's feet shift themselves into a fighting stance, although her hands stay at her sides. She should be afraid — the self-enclosed part of her brain notices this — but all the places that would feel fear are busy being angry. Across the street, at the edge of her vision, a cab pulls up.

"You okay?" the driver calls.

"Got a little disagreement here."

The driver slams out of his cab and takes a position on the sidewalk. Everything from the line of his neck to the jut of his belly says he wants a fight. Cath can't remember his name — Tom, maybe, or Tony. He's only been driving a few months, and he keeps to himself for the most part, working the radio, staying off the stands.

The passenger shifts back to keep from being caught

between Cath and whatever his name is, and they freeze there for a second like a water molecule springing outward as it turns to ice.

"I don't give a fuck how many of you there are," he says.

Cath takes this to mean Oh, shit, and it should please her, but it doesn't, somehow.

The woman in the cab slides across the back seat and opens the door a crack. Cath pushes it closed. She reaches through the front window and punches the button down.

"You stay in the cab."

The woman drops back against the seat, giving up, as if by pushing the button down Cath had locked her in. As if Cath had some authority over her. The woman's in her early twenties. She looks like she wouldn't take the garbage out without putting makeup on first.

Cath turns back to the men. They're pushing each other experimentally on the shoulder and brushing each other's hands away, edging themselves toward a fight. Tom or Tony—whoever he is—hasn't bothered to ask what the fight's about, so everything they say to each other is general: personal insults, dirty words, noise and static. They're evenly matched. The passenger's younger, taller, in better shape, but the driver's been brewing his anger longer. It'll scald his veins if he doesn't pour it out soon. The word *nigger* gets used, and the pushing gets heavier. The calm part of Cath's brain has stopped talking to her, and so has the rest of it. She has no thoughts and makes no decisions. The passenger pushes the driver backward, and she steps into the space between them and yells at them to knock it off.

A moment of startled calm explodes between them. It lasts long enough for Cath to think how odd all of this is. She turns toward the passenger.

"Just get the change, okay?"

"Fuck the change. Nobody calls me nigger."

"He's an idiot. Please, just go get the change."

Behind her, Tom's yelling, "You act like a nigger, I'll call you a nigger."

It takes a few seconds for Cath to unscramble what he's said from the sound of her own words. The passenger moves to the side, and Cath shifts with him.

"I want a fuckin' apology," he yells, pointing a long arm toward the other driver.

"Apology?" the driver bellows.

Over her shoulder, Cath yells at him to shut up.

"I'll give you a fuckin' apology."

Cath reaches a hand toward the passenger's arm. He yanks out of her reach.

"C'mere a minute. C'mere. Let me talk to you."

"You get out of there. This is between me and him."

"He's sorry, okay?"

"I'll tell you who's sorry."

The other driver bellows, "Sorry?"

Cath can't see the other driver, but the passenger moves to the side again. She turns so she has a shoulder to each man. She believes that standing between them is stupid and that the sheer stupidity of it will protect her. With a conscious effort, she lowers her voice.

"You," she says to the other driver, "this isn't your

fight and you're not helping, I want you out of it." She turns her back so she can pretend not to hear him. "Can we go over there and talk?" she says to the passenger.

She nods toward the back door of the bar, a few yards away. The front door's around the corner and out of sight, on Deele Street.

The passenger hesitates, but when Cath moves closer and puts a hand on his arm he doesn't shake her off. He moves with her, keeping his eyes on the other driver.

"Look," she says, "I'm sorry about this guy, really. Would you just go get the change, and we'll forget the whole thing?"

He shakes her hand off.

"You're sorry about him, hunh? You're sorry about him? You hadn't tried to be such a hardass, you wouldn't be standing there now apologizing for him."

He points at her as he talks, a long finger jabbing toward her, pulling back, jabbing again.

"Look—"

"No, you look. You started this thing, now you're fuckin' sorry about the way your boyfriend there runs it. Isn't that right? Isn't it?"

"Look—"

"I'll tell you who I want an apology from. You."

"Fine. You want an apology, you got an apology. Okay? You got an apology, right there. Now please, just get the goddamn change before the nutcase starts up again."

The passenger nods several times, measuring her words to make sure they're enough. They shouldn't be—Cath hasn't found the right tone for an apology—but he says, "All right, then," and opens the bar door. The smell of stale beer rolls over Cath and into the street. The door closes behind him, and Cath's left staring at a brown door, a white stucco wall, the stenciled words SAND BAR, until she feels foolish standing there and has to turn back to the other driver, who's leaning against the rear fender of her cab, arms crossed, looking like he didn't expect any better of a woman. Cath stops a yard away and crosses her own arms. She's starting to tremble.

"It's over, okay? I'd like you to go now."

She sounds like a bad actor who escaped from a parenting video: I'd like you to pick up your toys now; I'd like you to eat your beets now. Clear, assertive statements, delivered in a freeze-dried, reasonable voice. He doesn't twitch. Cath measures his weight against her own as if he were a car she had to push.

"You're going to get yourself hurt one day, lady."

"I'll deal with that when the time comes."

"I'd like to see it."

Cath waits. He waits. The trembling's stronger.

"I'll tell you a little secret about your Afro-American friend there. He doesn't like you. He never will like you. You might as well get used to that."

Cath should say something withering here but has to settle for a cold stare. He shifts his weight off the car, grins, then strolls to his cab.

Cath holds her ground until he turns the corner, then she sags against the front door. The passenger's still in the bar, finishing a beer to prove Cath can't rush him, or to calm his own shakes. The meter's running. She'll ask the supervisor to write off the difference when she pulls in. She could go into the bar after the passenger, but her only assurance that he won't disappear out the front door is the woman trapped in the back seat, and if Cath goes inside, even this woman may find the spirit to take off, leaving Cath with nothing.

Cath checks her watch. By the time her arms fold across each other again, she can't remember what it said. The wind blows leaves off a tree just down the street from the bar. The tree's golden, like a domesticated sunrise — compact, apartment sized. The sun's warm. The cab door's warm. A perfect Indian-summer day. Time passes. The meter's been running for years.

When the passenger finally does come back, he's strolling as easily as the other driver did. Men must practice this, looking like fighting and adrenaline don't affect them. He counts two dollars and sixty-five cents in nickels, dimes, and pennies into Cath's hand and tries the back door of the cab.

"Unlock the door," he yells to the woman. His voice is set at a level that blasts past the woman, out the far door and into the houses across the street. She pulls up on the button.

He holds the door for her, then points at Cath.

"You're in over your head, you know that?"

Cath holds her eyes steady and keeps her head from nodding in agreement. She watches them into the bar, the woman passing under the man's arm as he holds this door too.

Cath turns the meter off at five dollars and thirty-five cents, rolls the windows up, and locks the doors. The trembling's moved inward from her arms and legs. Her stomach and spine are bouncing it back and forth between them. The word *nigger* echoes in her head, picking up resonances she never knew were there, as if she were the one who'd used it. As if she'd turned it out into the world to begin with. She runs a hand down her arm, trying to scrape off the sludge it left behind.

She turns onto Deele Street and drives to McDonald's, where she buys coffee and an apple pie. The pie comes in a cardboard folder that looks like an escape pod in a science-fiction movie. She'd take her chances in an escape pod right now. She's pretty sure that whatever world she found would be an improvement. She slides into a chair and rests her forearms on the table. When her hands are easier to control, she'll open a container of cream and pour it into her coffee.

By the window a group of boys are poking each other in the shoulder and calling each other names, practicing being boys—or practicing being white boys. Cath's not sure how to unwrap one from the other. Do black boys this age shove each other differently?

Cath feels glaringly white, and she feels this as a limit. It limits what she knows. It limits who she knows and how she knows them. She's not used to thinking of herself this way, although she probably should be—all the information she needed has been there for years.

Cath's hands are no easier to control, but she opens the cream anyway and sips the coffee. She tips the escape pod so the pie's head emerges, testing the atmosphere to see if it will sustain life.

One boy calls another a dickhead.

The second says, "Who's a dickhead, dickhead?"

The first one reaches across the table and pushes the second one's forehead. They're a step away from being thrown out, and their friends pull them into their seats.

Cath bites into her pie. The word *nigger* ricochets off the curved sounding board of her skull, tunnels through gray matter, and strikes bone again just when she thinks she's rid of it. The boys are laughing. They're friends again. She shapes the word *nigger* silently. She rolls it into a ball until it's small and sticky enough that the letters lose their shape and with it their power to carry sound, meaning, pain. She condenses it until she's sure it's one piece of ugliness she can keep from the world. She does this with as much concentration as if the word weren't loose in the world already, as if by muffling every surface where it could strike an echo she could step so far outside the battle lines she's suddenly discovered that neither side would know her.

As solutions to the world's problems go, this is about as effective as the bumper stickers that tell people to visualize world peace, but it's all she can think of: a decision that if she doesn't know how to make the world better, she can at least try not to make it worse.

The boys by the window laugh. One of them throws his shoulder against the boy on the aisle, dumping him out of his seat. This boy hurls himself full force into the booth and the boy who pushed him. They laugh louder. One of them says, "Shh," and they giggle. They don't think they're making the world worse either, and maybe they're not. Even Tom, or whatever his name is, probably thinks he's a soldier in the battle for justice and the noble white race, or some damn thing. She could try to find out, but it would involve listening to him, and that's more of a sacrifice than she can face right now.

She takes another bite of her pie. *Captain's log: The world on which I have landed is populated by a race of large bipeds whose primitive level of civilization and aggressive tendencies, I confess, cause me some concern for my own safety. If anyone is able to retrieve these logs, I caution you to . . .*

Cath sips her coffee and asks herself what a person has to do to justify their presence on the earth, since visualizing world peace isn't going to cut it. The closest she can come to an answer is, *More than I'm doing.* That makes her uncomfortable, but she doesn't wink out of existence.

Résumé

Name: Catherine Anne Rahven

Age: 28

Previous Employment: Waited tables at an Italian restaurant where the cook kept a pint of whiskey under the counter and yelled at her if she came in to pick up an order before it was ready. And if she wasn't there to take it the minute it was up. He yelled when she said she'd ordered two lasagnas, not three — the third was supposed to be spaghetti. The manager fired her four separate times for making the cook mad. Each time, he called the next day and asked where the hell she was, she was late for work. The fourth time, she said she'd be right in, took the phone off the hook, and ran herself a bath.

Waited tables in a Chinese restaurant where she wore a linen-supply company's idea of a Chinese dress — high neck, tight skirt, cloth buttons — and got yelled at by four sets of cooks in two different languages.

Waited tables in a steak house where a businessman asked her name and age and put his tip into her hand like they were doing something dirty.

Delivered phone books.

Currently driving cab.

Education: Bachelor of Social Work; GPA 3.5

Other Activities: Published five short stories, mostly in magazines no one but twelve other writers will ever read. Allegedly writing a mystery. Searching for work. Waiting for her real life to begin.

Who to Notify in Case of Emergency: Cath wishes she knew.

The Part of This Moment That Isn't Hers

"What if you had one sentence to sum up the kind of woman you'd like to be with," Tavi says. "What would it be?"

Cath twitches her lips as if she's in pain. They're sitting at Tavi's kitchen table while Tavi's lover, Jean, fusses over a huge pot of soup.

It's Cath's fault that they're talking about the kind of woman she'd like to be with—she's the one who said she was lonely. She can't remember now why she said it, but she knows she was stating a fact, not trying to change it.

"It doesn't work that way," Cath says. "You don't draw up a list and then find someone who fits it. You get attracted to someone and hope to hell it works out."

Tavi tucks the pencil behind her ear. She has intensely curly hair, and a slash of sunlight slips across it every time she moves her head, reaching down through it the way sunlight reaches through water. Cath's eyes follow it, measuring the distance between surface and scalp. Her own hair lies flat and dull against her head. She turns to look out the closed window.

"Maybe that's what's been wrong," Tavi says.

"If I'm attracted to the wrong kind of woman, then I'm going to draw up the wrong list, aren't I?"

"Not if you set out to change that side of your life, no."

Outside the window, Michelle, Tavi's daughter, and a friend of hers are sitting on a swing set, pushing against the ground with their feet so they sway back and forth as they talk. They're at the far edge of childhood—too old for swings but young enough still to hang around the backyard wishing they were somewhere else. In Cath's right ear, Tavi's talking about changing the pattern of Cath's relationships by making them conscious. She asks what could be more conscious than placing a classified ad, and she keeps on talking without waiting for an answer. Cath tries to remember what she talked about with her friends when she was Michelle's age, but all she remembers is the shifting patterns of intensity and boredom, longing and hurt.

Cath cuts into Tavi's monologue and asks when she's supposed to have time for all this, although the truth is she does have time—she graduated at the end of the summer session and has a piece of paper with fancy lettering to prove it.

"You make time," Jean says over the sound of running water in the sink. "Like everybody else."

She's scrubbing a carrot with a brown, health-food-looking brush. Her sleeves are rolled up past her elbows. It's cold in the house—it's too early in the fall to turn the heat on but not warm enough to be comfortable without it. Cath's wearing a heavy sweater. The girls outside are wearing oversized sweatshirts.

Jean turns the water off and lays two carrots on the cutting board. She slices them, rocking the knife evenly

89

on its tip so it cuts like a machine — a paper cutter; a guillotine. During the week Jean works as a cook. On weekends she cooks for the people Tavi gathers around her but keeps her distance from them. Food's her bridge to the world. Tavi does the entertaining, organizes dishwashing brigades, sends people home with soup, stew, slices of bread and pie. It's a strange relationship, but it seems to suit them.

The soup breathes out a steam of chicken, vegetables, herbs Cath can't name but recognizes as comforting. Jean carries carrot slices to the pot on the flat side of the knife.

"Let's try this another way," Tavi says. "What kind of things do you like to do? You know, movies, softball, long walks by the river —"

Tavi has the pencil in her hands again, and she's rolling it up and down her chin while she waits for an answer.

"I can't do this," Cath says. "It's too cold-blooded."

Jean lifts a corner of the towel that covers her bread dough to see how it's rising. Her hair is like Cath's — short, flat, nondescript. She's rounder than Tavi, and taller.

"I think it's sexy to say out in the open like that that you're available," she says.

"It's not sexy, it's pitiful."

Tavi's holding the pencil just above her chin, under her lip. It looks odd but thoughtful. It occurs to Cath to ask if Tavi and Jean knew what they were looking for before they met, but before the words reach her mouth the kitchen door slams open and Michelle comes in leading a toddler in a ruffled sweatshirt and pants. The girl's old enough to walk well but still more a baby than a child. Between two and three, Cath thinks, but she doesn't spend enough time around kids to be sure. She's a small child, thin every place she isn't diapered.

Michelle's friend stands behind them, by the door, trying to make herself invisible.

"Who's this?" Tavi asks. She sets her pencil on the table and kneels down, holding a finger out for the baby to grab. "Where'd you come from?"

Her voice is high and bright, an adult-talking-to-baby voice.

"She just came in the yard," Michelle says. "We were sitting on the swings."

Jean says, "Oh, shit."

Tavi picks the baby up and coos at her, "Are you lost, sweetheart? Did you get lost?"

The baby squinches up her face and cries.

"You're scaring her," Michelle says.

Tavi lets Michelle take the baby back and set her on the floor, but now that she's started crying she keeps on, feet planted squarely on the linoleum, tears running down her cheeks.

"Can she talk?" Jean asks.

"I don't know."

Michelle takes the baby's hand and says, "Where's Mommy? Where'd Mommy go?"

The baby wails. Michelle picks her up and coos nonsense at her. Her voice has a different pitch than Tavi's, higher and flatter. Tavi adopted Michelle when she was six, and there's no reason their voices should sound the same, but the difference between them surprises Cath anyway.

"Did you look for her parents?" Jean asks over the baby's hiccuping cries.

Michelle rolls her eyes toward the ceiling. She and Jean don't like each other—Jean never wanted to be a parent, and if Michelle ever wanted a second parent, Jean wasn't what she had in mind. Jean rents an apartment three blocks away and only spends weekends here, but even so it's not easy for any of them.

"Well did you?"

"Yes, we looked."

Michelle comes down hard on *yes* when she says this, turning it into something insulting.

"In the alley or in front?"

"Both, duh."

"Shell, don't talk that way," Tavi says.

"What way?"

"You know what way."

The baby wails out long, gasping shreds of sound.

Jean sets a wooden spoon down as if the final bit of evidence just weighed in. Cath can't remember how the spoon got into her hand.

"I'm calling the cops."

"Give us a minute here," Tavi says. "Wherever her parents are, they'll have Child Protection on their heads the minute you call."

"Maybe they should have Child Protection on their heads."

"It can happen to anyone. You turn your back for two seconds—"

"So where are they? They should be out there screaming their lungs out for her. For god's sake, Tav, the next thing you know we'll have someone on the doorstep screaming we kidnapped her."

Tavi pushes her chair into the table as if everything's been settled.

"Shell, you and Amanda sit out front with her in case someone's looking. I'll try the alley. Cath, you try over on Fourth."

Cath walks as far as the alley with Tavi and then starts to jog. The baby's wail fades away behind the houses.

The only thing moving on Fourth Avenue is a boy riding a plastic tricycle along the sidewalk. He sits low in the seat and his feet stretch out in front to reach the peddles. Cath blocks his path.

"Did you see anyone looking for a lost child? A little girl—a baby?"

The boy looks up at her. She's every stranger he's been warned not to talk to.

"Did you?"

He shakes his head, keeping to the letter of the law by clamping his jaws shut, and Cath steps aside for him, but instead of riding forward he stands with one foot on either side of the bike, lifts it, and waddles a half circle so he can ride back to his own front walk, where nothing like this has ever happened to him. No one else is out—not a dog, not a single frantic parent, no adults who might know the child. An old blue pickup drives past. Cath raises an arm at the last minute to flag it down, but the driver cruises by, not seeing, not understanding, or not caring. She yells "Hey" after him and stands still to watch him disappear.

She jogs back toward Tavi's. She's not sure why she doesn't walk, but it seems important to bring them the news that she has no news as quickly as possible.

Michelle is on the steps with the baby on her lap. The child's stopped crying and has a ball that someone's found for her. An older woman's joined them — gray haired, lipsticked, and wearing powder blue knit slacks.

"Nothing," Cath says to Tavi. She's breathing hard and feels a little foolish about it. Everyone else looks relaxed.

"She's a mystery," Tavi says to the older woman.

"She must be visiting someone or live on another block," the woman says. "I've never seen her before."

"I told Jean to go ahead and call the police," Tavi says to Cath. "Someone should have been looking for her by now."

"Maybe the mother's one of these drug addicts you hear about," the neighbor says. "You just don't know, the way things are these days."

"She's not," Michelle says. "She just lost her, that's all."

She bounces the baby on her knees, drawing the girl's attention away from the words she doesn't understand yet.

"It could happen to anyone."

When Michelle stops bouncing her, the baby raises her arm and throws the ball onto the walk. She's sober faced, like someone working out a problem — no crowing or clapping. The ball rolls onto the grass and stops there. Michelle's friend picks it up and holds it out to the baby. Both girls bend toward her as intently as if this would keep her from being alone in the world. They're building a family for her, casting themselves as the adults, even if the family only holds together for a few more minutes.

"Look at the poor little thing," the neighbor says. "Who could let a child that tiny wander off alone? When you think of the people who might have found her —"

The baby accepts the ball and throws it again. Cath picks it up and hands it to Michelle's friend to give back. She still doesn't know what she wants in a lover, but what she wants in her life is exactly the part of this moment that isn't hers: the whole thorny tangle of family, even if it includes Michelle and Jean wishing each other into oblivion and a neighbor on the sidelines, sentimental and scandalized.

Starting Over

"Lyle Sexton knew cab driving was dangerous," Cath writes.

She crosses this out. Under it, she writes, "Flora tells the police that when they were still married he used to say people exaggerated the danger of driving cab. She cries when she talks about him."

She draws a line under this and tries again.

"North Port was known for its cold winters and its general level of civility. It called itself the Livable City, as if all around the country other cities had been boarded up and abandoned."

She skips a line and writes, "So?"

She decides the name Sexton sounds fake and writes a list of other possibilities: Polanski, Greenberg, Semple, Sanchez, McCreary.

"Lyle Sanchez McCreary was having a bad day," she writes, "and getting shot through the head didn't improve it."

She doesn't bother to cross this out. It will remind her that she knew she was writing trash, which will make everything else she writes on this set of pages — no matter how bad it gets — less painful to reread.

"It was a dark and stormy night," she writes.

She draws a line.

"Lyle Greenberg was found in the front seat of his cab three hours after his shift should have ended. The force of the bullet that killed him had thrown him forward, onto the steering wheel."

She crosses out "onto the steering wheel." That's where she'll insert some knockout phrase that will make the scene jump off the page.

All she needs is the knockout phrase.

Ice

Cath has sixty-eight dollars on her trip sheet when she parks along the River Road to eat her sandwich. She has twelve dollars and fifteen cents in scale, which is what drivers call tips plus anything they happen to steal. Of that, six dollars and fifty-five cents came from a package run that she didn't put on the meter, and the rest is legal. She's kept track of this on the back of a receipt card. This is her last day of driving, and already she misses it. She misses the way drivers lean against the side of a cab in good weather, killing time while they wait for a run, and she misses the dispatcher begging for someone to pick up a laundromat run that keeps calling back; she misses the freedom to slide her seat back and look down at the Mississippi, trusting that sooner or later someone else will pick up the woman at the laundromat and drive her the six miserable blocks to her apartment.

It's early winter, and the river's low. On the far side, at the base of the bluff, a snow-covered beach stretches south to the freeway bridge. In the spring the water will come up to the trees, and the beach will disappear.

Cath's been watching this river for as long as she can remember. The city draws its water upstream and deposits its sewage downstream, so the river's flowed through her all her life, and she through it. She'll miss seeing it every day.

She turns the engine off, and the cab cools down, but the sun pouring in through the driver's-side windows keeps it comfortable. She eats her sandwich—peanut butter on whole wheat—and when it's gone she calls in her location. The dispatcher gives her a liquor store for someone named Matt.

Matt turns out to be an old man who makes his way painfully toward the cab, carrying a paper bag the size of a six-pack. Cath gets out and opens the door for him. By the time he lines himself up with the seat and lowers himself in so she can shut the door, her fingers are freezing.

She drives Matt to an apartment building—light-colored brick, windows that open sideways, built quick and cheap during the sixties. She turns the meter arm to nine o'clock.

"Two ninety-five."

Matt hands her a single dollar bill.

"You're not going to like this, but that's all I have."

He opens his wallet to show her how empty it is, and she looks into it and thinks about driving him somewhere else and dumping him. She thinks about screaming at him and about checking his pockets to see what he's got squirreled away, but whatever force drives people to do these things has walked off the job already, leaving her empty even of anger.

She opens her door, then his, and takes the paper bag.

"I'll keep this."

"That's only fair. You have a right to do that."

He shakes his head to let her know how disappointing he is, and the rest of the human race along with him.

The bag's heavy in Cath's hand. If this happened to Lyle McCreary Polanski, he'd damn well know what to do about it. Every driver she's ever known is shrieking at her to ask why the hell the old man called a cab when he knew he was broke, and why he bought beer instead of saving money for the fare. They don't expect her to do any more than that—he's an old man, after all, and she's a woman—but she owes it to everyone to chew him out.

The questions are reasonable. The problem is that she knows the answers: He called a cab because he wanted to go home; he bought beer because he wanted to drink it; he isn't going to pay because she came along too late in the sequence. You have money and you buy something and then you don't have money—it's gone, that simply.

Matt makes his slow way up the walk to the building. She sets the bag beside her on the seat and assembles the story into something she can imagine telling in the drivers' room. It ends with *So I took his six-pack,* which she'll set on the counter and distribute to whoever's around, skipping Joe Addison if he's there because he's started going to AA meetings. They'll pop the tabs and agree that it wasn't a bad trade, all told. They'll wish her luck in her new job and tell her she's smart to get out—it's a loser's game, cab driving. They'll go to the bar for one last round before she's really out of the business.

She starts the cab and pulls away. Matt's still creeping between the low snowbanks toward his front door. He moves slower than anyone she can ever remember. She won't tell the drivers she feels like a sucker, and they won't tell her that she is one. It's an agreement they all have. Nothing they can do leaves them feeling like they got their own back, and so none of them mention this.

She brakes for the stop sign at the corner, turns right, and bids on a call that's gone wild. She pulls to the curb, writes the address on her trip sheet, and lifts the paper bag toward her to see what brand Matt bought her for a going-away present.

What Matt bought her is a plastic bag of ice. She puts the cab into park, slides her seat back, and pounds the back of her skull once, neatly, against the headrest. She picks up the mike.

"Dispatch."

"Go ahead, twenty-one."

"I've got to give you that Thirty-Fourth Street back."

"What's the problem?"

"It's a long story. Let's just say I got a pickup."

"Let's just say, hunh?"

"It's as close as we're going to get, okay?"

By way of an answer, the dispatcher calls the stand again. Cath leans across the seat to open the passenger door and heaves the bag into the gutter. Then she turns off the radio, slides her seat forward, and heads for the garage.

The Force of Gravity

Cath steps out of her car into a puddle of slush that's disguised itself as gray December street snow. She's wearing the thin-soled black shoes she bought for job interviews, and they absorb slush as neatly as if they'd been designed just for that. She could probably have gotten by with something more casual today, but this is her first day on the new job—her first day as a social worker—and she's not sure what they expect.

She rings the doorbell and waits. Her right shoe is soaked through. When it dries it'll show a salt mark at the high-water line. If the bathrooms have paper towels, she'll wet one and try to rub it out.

She wonders if she should ring a second time.

She can't picture herself rubbing salt off her shoe without feeling sneaky about it, like she's hiding some character flaw. Or trying to.

She's pulling a hand out of her pocket to ring again when the door opens partway and her new boss fills the opening. Cath makes an awkward gesture, half a wave, with the hand that was reaching for the bell.

Her new boss is tall, fiftyish, and soft voiced. She bends forward at the shoulders like she's spent her life apologizing for her height. She's called Neddie, short for Cath has no idea what: Annette, Theodora,

Nanette, Nadine. Cath stands a step below her, waiting for the door to swing back, and is struck by the conviction that she's too short for this job, and too young. Nothing they taught her in school will be any use here. She's had, what? four months since they gave her a diploma? Shouldn't she be wiser by now?

Neddie gawks at Cath and says, "Oh my god" twice, then, "Come in."

Cath steps inside, bringing the top of her head level with Neddie's shoulder. She's still too short, although everyplace else she's been in her life she was average height. She tells herself that she *was* hired, she remembers being hired, it's not something she could have misunderstood. She has a moment of panic about having quit at the cab company if this job's going to disappear before it ever starts, and she closes the door behind herself. Neddie says "Oh my god" again, then, "I'm sorry, you're not who I expected. I forgot all about you."

She spreads her hands helplessly, drawing Cath's eyes to the entryway they're standing in and the coats hanging on pegs along its walls.

"I could—" Cath says, not sure yet what she could. She hesitates, then says, "come back later?"

Neddie glances over her shoulder, toward the interior of the house, then turns back to Cath.

"No, please. We've had—" She spreads her hands again. "Would you mind waiting for me?"

Before Cath can answer, Neddie corrects herself.

"That's the wrong question. Actually, it's not a question at all. You'll have to wait for me."

Cath follows Neddie to the office where she inter-
viewed for the job. She sits in a chair beside Neddie's
desk as carefully as if she were at the bank applying for
a loan, and Neddie grabs a ragged assortment of papers
off a shelf and hands them to her. Her desk is buried in
papers — some stacked, others layered like ancient
cities, waiting for an archeologist to sift one era from
the next.

"If you want to read through these —" She looks
back to the shelf for more paper but doesn't spot anything she likes. "They'll give you some of the history —"

Cath picks up the top one obediently. It has photos,
print, Gothic letters that spell out River House. She
absorbs nothing.

"We've had a suicide," Neddie says. "I'm really
sorry."

And then she's gone. Cath turns pages, replaying
the last couple of minutes but saying all the right things
this time. Minutes pass; geological ages pass. From another part of the house, a woman's voice rises in a howl,
breaks into a sob, and trails off. Cath turns more pages.
Eventually the words begin to make sense.

Most of what she's holding are grant proposals, one
for money to finish the attic, adding six extra rooms —
twelve more residents — and another to fund an intern-
ship program for residents to work at local businesses
and organizations. They explain River House as a
transitional housing program for the homeless and for
those who would otherwise become homeless; they say
it provides a safe, chemically free environment where
residents can stabilize their lives before moving on to

independent living. Cath memorized this for her first interview, but she reads it as if she'd never seen it before and had a test coming up.

More time passes. She begins to think she'll spend her whole first day forgotten in this office. She'll draw her first paycheck before Neddie comes to collect her.

The door opens, and she looks up, expecting Neddie, but the head in the doorway is younger and about on the level where Cath's would appear. The curve of one ear is outlined by a row of colored studs. The head's followed by a body in torn jeans and a black sweater. The woman introduces herself as Mary Elizabeth, and the name's so primly at odds with the jeans and earrings that Cath almost laughs.

Mary Elizabeth looks around the office as if she can't make up her mind whether to come in or stay out.

"Neddie asked me to rescue you. Come have a cup of coffee, why don't you. I feel like I ought to be available out there in case anyone needs me."

Cath sets her stack of papers on the chair and waits for Mary Elizabeth to lead her out of the desert, but Mary Elizabeth doesn't; she balances her weight against the door's swaying edge, leaning into the room.

"Neddie told you what happened?"

Cath nods. Whatever she decided was the right thing to say, it's gotten away from her already.

"You can leave your purse and stuff here."

Mary Elizabeth sets the door so it will lock after them. Cath hasn't carried a purse in years—not since she started driving cab. All she has with her is her coat, which she bought for job interviews at the same time she bought the shoes. Her cap and scarf are jammed into the sleeves. None of this is worth explaining, and instead she says thanks and follows Mary Elizabeth.

In the living room Cath catches a glimpse of a man sitting on the floor, curled forward and sobbing, while another man sits on the couch, his legs bracing the first man's back and his hands massaging his shoulders. Gay men, both of them. They're too graceful to be straight, and too easy about touch.

Neddie appears from a corner of the room that Cath can't see and kneels beside the sobbing man. Cath follows Mary Elizabeth into the dining room without hearing what Neddie's about to say, but she's convinced it will be the simplest possible question: Are you okay?

In the dining room, Cath and Mary Elizabeth fill mugs with coffee. Cath's is blue and says NORTH STAR PET CLINIC. Mary Elizabeth's says LET'S GO DANCING.

The dining room's an odd mix: restaurant meets rec room; the late-nineteenth century collides with the late-twentieth; poverty inherits from wealth as soon as the things wealth once owned don't signify wealth anymore. There's a lesson in this somewhere. Six tables are crammed into the dining room of what was once a small mansion. Dark wood paneling covers the lower half of the walls — the real thing, direct from some old-growth tropical forest. No do-it-yourself-store wood-grain paneling here. The tables are mismatches that must have come from the kitchens and basements of church members all over town.

Cath follows Mary Elizabeth toward two women at

a formica table. They could almost be sisters — they're wide, solid, straight haired, and they have the same expressionless face that Neddie had when she opened the front door. It's not a look Cath's had a category for, but she's starting to recognize it: It's the look a steer gets in the slaughterhouse just after the hammer lands on its forehead but before the brain disconnects from the heart so that it falls. It knows something's happened, and it knows it's bad, but it doesn't have time to sort out what the hell it is.

Mary Elizabeth asks how they're doing — it's more a greeting than a question — and they nod blankly: They're alive; their hearing works.

"Is he still up there?" one of them whispers, and Mary Elizabeth says yeah, he is, but it shouldn't be long now.

Cath and Mary Elizabeth sit at a back table and stare into their coffee mugs as if something wildly important were going on inside them.

"I'm sorry, but I'm damned if I know what to say to you," Mary Elizabeth says. "This is all — "

"Yeah. I can understand that."

"The thing is, I was up there. There's blood everywhere, like he was going out of his way to spread it around."

She looks back into her mug to make sure everything's okay in there.

"I don't know, maybe he was. Going out of his way, I mean. Maybe that made sense to him. You want to know what's nuts? The first thing I thought when I saw it was that he should have been more considerate. As if,

I don't know, as if he'd spilled some cereal or something and not bothered to sweep it up."

She looks up from her mug.

"I'll tell you the truth. I'm so mad at him right now I'd kill him myself if he weren't already dead."

She tries to laugh and produces an odd, shaky sound instead.

Cath's mother has a stock of phrases to meet disasters with — *God, what next? How could anybody do that?* — and Cath hears them now, playing quietly in her head. She says, "Does anyone know why?" and it comes out in her mother's voice.

Mary Elizabeth shakes her head.

"He'd only been here a few days. The thing is, he shouldn't have been here at all. It's down in black and white — we don't take anyone who's a danger to others or a suicide risk. We're not set up for that, and it's not open to interpretation. The intake worker should've screened him out in the first five minutes of the interview. It's the most basic thing there is. You see anyone that serene, like they've made their peace with the world, all the alarms should go off. Every one of them."

Cath files this away and attaches a question to it: How serene does a person have to be to set off alarms? Does she have to lose someone before she learns the signs?

"There's even blood on the ceiling," Mary Elizabeth says. "How the hell'd he get it on the ceiling?"

Neither of them has touched their coffee. Cath runs a finger around the handle of her mug. The doorbell rings, and Cath follows Mary Elizabeth to the door.

She feels like a little sister, dragging along behind the older kids, but she can't face sitting alone again. She wishes Mary Elizabeth would tell her to come with her, or find something useful for her to do. She'd like more than this, actually: a written invitation, maybe; a press pass; a name tag she could hang on her shirt saying she has a reason to be here, she's not just gawking.

Mary Elizabeth lets in two men with a stretcher and points the way upstairs, but she stops at the base of the stairs and looks after them. Neddie comes out of the living room and touches Cath on the shoulder.

"I'm so sorry you had to start today."

Cath smiles. She wants to say it's okay. She feels the words forming in her throat and knows that all they mean is *Stay here; keep talking to me,* but before they have time to gather any breath behind them Neddie follows the men upstairs. Cath turns to Mary Elizabeth instead and nods toward the second floor.

"Shouldn't we see if there's anything we can do?"

"She wants everyone to stay as far away from the room as possible."

Something about this bothers Cath, but she's not sure what. People start to gather at the foot of the stairs, coming from the living room, the basement, the offices, drawn by the same gravitational force that draws people's eyes toward traffic accidents.

Gravity may also explain how quiet they are—it's too strong for sound to escape. If it were any stronger, it would suck in light and they'd all be invisible. This absence of human speech is what finally makes the situation real for Cath, and what makes her realize that it hasn't seemed real before. Someone's dead here. Not all that long before she rang the doorbell, he was alive. Now he isn't. The silence is a weight on her lungs, something she has to press against to draw breath.

The men reappear with the stretcher. One corner knocks against the wall when they turn the corner of the stairs, and they have to back up, raise the end, and try again. The crowd parts to let them through, and everyone turns to watch them to the door. Nothing anywhere matters as much as this does. Even after the men and the stretcher are gone, they keep on looking at the place where the stretcher last was instead of drifting back to the rooms they came from.

A long moment passes—a minute, five minutes, half a minute. Gravity distorts the flow of time. Neddie comes downstairs, walking heavily. She says quietly and to no one in particular, "We'll have to clean it somehow. We'll have to get it all clean."

No one answers. Cath wants to tell her that cold water takes blood out of almost anything. The pressure behind the information is almost more than she can hold back. The only thing that keeps her from saying it is the weight of the silence outside her. She's half convinced that no other woman in the house knows about cold water and blood and that everything will be manageable if she can only tell them.

More time pours out meaninglessly before Neddie says, "There's no point all of us standing here when we could sit in the living room."

It's a moment before the crowd shifts its weight. Cath has time to realize that for the most part she can't sort these people into staff and residents — they could be anything and anyone. They're as much alike as drops of water. She's the only oil in the mix, and she hesitates to follow them.

Neddie steps down off the lowest stair and stands in front of Cath.

"I want to meet with the group, and I have to call his family — and a few members of the board. Then I'll be with you."

"Whenever you want."

Neddie runs a finger over the dark wooden panelling and studies it.

"I wish I knew what I'm going to say to them."

She says this to herself, to the rich, dark wood. Cath opens her mouth and shuts it, and Neddie seems to shake herself awake.

"That's not your problem. This isn't — " She looks around. "We're none of us like this, really. These are extraordinary circumstances."

Cath's cup is still in the dining room. She dumps out the cold coffee, refills it, and carries it to the only occupied table, where a man sits staring at his clasped hands. She asks if she can sit with him, and he loosens one hand to gesture at the three empty chairs, then locks it back into the other and studies the pair of them. In the living room a woman's loud, flat voice says, "I told him last night, 'If you're going to walk down the hallway here, you have to tie your robe closed. Whatever you've got under there, I don't want to know about it.'"

Another voice answers, but Cath can't make it out.

The sliding doors between the living room and dining room are closed. All she can hear of the other voices is their music, not their sense.

"You think I was wrong to tell him that?" the first woman asks. "You think I shouldn't have said anything?"

The other voices lap over hers. They make comforting sounds. They tell her it's not her fault. They tell the living they can go ahead and live.

"I'm Cath Rahven," Cath says to the man's bent head. "I just started today. I'm on staff."

The man looks up. He has black hair and the steer-in-the-slaughterhouse look on his face.

"Dallas," he whispers.

Cath nods as if this makes sense to her, then asks, "Your name or where you're from?"

"I'm from New Jersey."

They listen to the wash of voices in the other room.

"I let that man die," Dallas whispers across the table to her. "I should have seen it coming."

"You didn't know it would happen."

She isn't quite whispering, but she's close. It's eerier than if they were screaming.

"We're supposed to know something. We're supposed to know something that's going to help people."

They both stare at his interlocked hands. Cath whispers, "It's not your fault," and the words become part of the silence between them. The voices in the next room lap at the closed doors.

Lifetimes later, Neddie puts her head through the doorway and says, "Dallas, come talk to me."

He rises like a man underwater and wades after her.

Cath wanders to the wall and reads chore lists — who cleans what when. She reads a flyer from a neighborhood health clinic. If Dallas didn't know how to keep the dead man alive, she sure as hell wouldn't. She doesn't know how to keep anyone else alive, either, or find them a job, a home, a moment of safety. By the time Neddie calls her name, she's reading a bus schedule and calculating the wait between buses. The predictability of this is comforting. So is its irrelevance.

She follows Neddie into her office, picks up the stack of proposals she left on the chair, and sits with them on her lap. Dallas must have done the same thing, and set them back when he left.

"I have a welcoming speech I usually make to new staff," Neddie says, "but I don't think I can manage it today. Let's just settle for this: We do the best we can here, but we can't keep anyone alive if they want to be dead, and we can't erase people's histories so they can start again with a decent chance this time. You want to hang on to those?"

It's a few seconds before Cath understands that Neddie's talking about the proposals. She hands them back, and Neddie dumps them on the far edge of her desk.

"People come here with problems you wouldn't believe," Neddie says half to Cath and half to the stacks of paper that surround her. "Mental illness, physical illness, abuse, addiction, alcoholism, bad luck, all of the above, any combination of the above, sometimes complicated by plain old rotten judgment and/or criminal behavior." She focuses fully on Cath. "You do the best you can, you don't let yourself think you're better than they are, and you don't let yourself think you're God. Any questions?"

"Seems clear enough."

"It's never clear enough. Let's get some forms filled out."

Neddie ruffles through a stack of folders. She's a comforting presence—tall, gentle, magnificently disorganized. Cath sits back in her chair and draws a breath that feeds every cell in her lungs. The worst has already happened. This shouldn't make her feel safe, but it does. From here on, it's a free ride.

Success Story

The first client Cath's scheduled to meet with is a man Neddie introduced her to yesterday, Hersh Millhouse. Cath was introduced to a lot of people yesterday and doesn't remember most of them, but Hersh stood out. In the emotional backwash of the suicide, when everyone else drew together, he kept himself separate—closed up tight enough that no one even tried to draw him in.

Hersh's file says he worked in a warehouse until he hurt his back. His workman's comp has run out, and he's been turned down for disability. The file says he claims to be in constant pain.

Cath can't prove his pain any more than he can, but she believes it's there. It's carved itself on his face, which is narrow and heavily lined. It's written in the way he holds himself as he walks through the door.

It's when he walks through the door that Cath should say something to start them talking, but he carries his separateness like a shield. The best she can think of is, "Cold in here, isn't it?"

The office is cold. It has a row of windows facing the street, and they smuggle warm air out to exchange on the street for huge amounts of cold. If there were a way to make money on the deal, they could fund Cath's salary.

Not that it would take much to do that.

Hersh gives her a grunt that might mean yeah, it is cold, and he works his way into a straight-backed chair, one hand on his cane and one against the wall for support. Cath watches until he's almost seated, then closes the door and drops into her own chair. She picks up his file.

"What I'd like to do as a way of getting to know each other is ask you to tell me about your goals."

A wave of anger slams through the air between them like the shock wave from an explosion.

"You want to see if the old dog remembers his tricks?"

Cath frowns. Goals are the heart of what River House does. The client and the social worker both have to agree to them, and the client's accountable for making progress toward them. It's what River House demands in return for food and shelter.

She repeats Hersh's words to herself, but they seem to be in some other language. More than a graceful amount of time limps past.

"Excuse me?"

"You want to know if I remember what my goals are supposed to be? You want to hear me recite them?"

"Nothing like that—"

"I could recite the Pledge of Allegiance too if you want to hear it."

The stiff cover of Hersh's file bends under Cath's spread hands. A host of cab drivers gathers in her head, condensing heavily into anger. She was trying to ask Hersh an open-ended goddamn question, she explains to them. That's what she was taught to do in Social Work Practice. You never ask a yes/no question unless you want yes/no information. You state the question in a way that allows the client the greatest possible latitude. No one warned her not to piss the client off in the process, and it probably wouldn't have helped if they had. No one told her what to do now that she has.

"If I said anything to offend you, I'm sorry," she says stiffly. "That's not what I meant to do."

Hersh leans forward an inch, one hand on the head of his cane to keep it from falling.

"What you meant matters about as much as piss in a rainstorm."

He puts a heavy emphasis on *meant*, making it sound like a strange word to have chosen, and nods at the file in Cath's lap.

"You read that yet?"

"Yeah, I read it."

"Then you read my goals, right?"

"I thought it'd be a good time to review them, that's all. Give us a way to get to know each other a little."

The pain has dropped away from Hersh's face and anger flows through him as cleanly as joy.

"Us," he says. "You want to talk about your goals too?"

"I've been concentrating on finding a job. Now I'm here, I'm not sure what comes next."

Hersh snorts at her.

"You people sit in your chairs with your papers on your laps, and you ask about a man's life like you never heard the word privacy. You know how many social workers I've had since I wrecked this back? Five of them, and every damn one wanted to get to know me. You want to tell me how come I'm so popular all of a sudden?"

The cab drivers in Cath's head crowd tighter. They're ready to tell Hersh just how popular he really is. Cath wonders how come she's got this bunch for an advisory council when what she needs is a committee of social workers.

She opens her mouth to say something, but Hersh cuts her off.

"And not one of them would've crossed the damn street to say hello before I landed on their caseload. Still wouldn't if they saw me anywhere but in their offices."

Hersh settles carefully against the hard back of his chair. His attention draws inward to track the pain this sets off.

"Look, we're more or less stuck with each other," Cath says when his attention surfaces again. "You got something you want to know about me, go ahead and ask."

"You don't get it, do you? I ask you something, it's because you let me. You ask me something, it's because you have a right to, and if I want to stay here I damn well better answer it."

Cath opens her mouth and closes it. She wants to tell him she's not like that, but it doesn't matter what she's like. He's right—if he doesn't give her something to write in the space marked *progress*, someone will decide he's not moving toward his goals, and he'll be history.

118

"Look, this is the first time I've ever done this, and I'm an idiot," she says. "Jesus I'm sorry."

He doesn't ask whether *this* means insult a client or interview one. He nods once, and Cath takes this as acceptance. They stare past each other at opposite corners of the room. Cath's corner holds the file cabinet and on top of it a dead plant that might once have been a poinsettia. Now it's a collection of sticks and ribbon in a foil-wrapped pot.

"How old are you, anyway?" he asks.

The anger's gone out of his voice and left it exhausted.

"Twenty-eight."

"Jesus."

"It's not something I can help."

"Then let me tell you a couple things about the world, all right? Before I hurt my back, I had a life of my own, same as you do. I went to work every day, I went home most nights, I didn't owe nothing to nobody, and I didn't answer to them either. Just like you, right? You think you're different than me?"

In a low voice, Cath says no, she's no different.

"One accident," Hersh says. "One goddamn accident and the whole world treats you like you messed up your head instead of your back. You can't work, and suddenly you get people half your age asking about progress toward your goals. You don't have a life anymore. You've got social workers, and you've got pain. You want to know what keeps me going? Spite, that's what. Knowing they want me dead."

Cath's lost again, and she frowns, shaking her head.

119

"Social Security, the whole lot of them. They think if they turn me down long enough, I'll crawl off and die somewhere and they can keep their money. That's what keeps me alive — goddamn Republicans."

"Is there anything you can do about the pain?" Cath's voice comes out almost as a whisper, like an echo of Dallas whispering across the table at her yesterday. She wonders if this is how you begin to lose a client, with this whispering, but whatever else she could say about Hersh, he doesn't look like a man who's made his peace. "Maybe a pain-management class?"

"Been there. Done that. I manage the pain, and the pain manages me right back."

Cath fingers the edge of the file.

"What do you want me to write under progress?"

"Tell them I called Social Security to check on my appeal."

Cath opens the file and writes this.

"You done with me?"

Cath says yeah. She tells him again that she's sorry.

"It's all happened before. Don't let it keep you up nights."

He works his way out of the chair. Cath's eyes fasten on his cane — polished black wood with an S-shaped handle, something he must've bought before the money ran out, when he still had a life. She tries to imagine him as the man who didn't want to be seen leaning on a hospital-issue adjustable cane. She opens the door for him.

"The guy they carried out of here yesterday," he says at the door. "I don't suppose you know his name."

"'Fraid not."

"Teddy something. I don't suppose you could look it up for me."

Cath rubs a hand across her forehead.

"Without the last name, I wouldn't know where to start, but even if I found it, I'd be violating his confidentiality if I told you."

"Mighta known," he says. "A person dies, it seems like somebody ought to remember their name, and here I can't. That's all I heard him called was Teddy."

"One of the residents oughta know, don't you think?"

Hersh doesn't bother to answer this. He doesn't remind her how crazy it is that she has to keep secret what she's sure everyone already knows. He says, "Poor dumb bastard did just what they wanted him to. A success story. No more cash down that rat hole. I'd give a lot to remember him by name, though."

Cath says again that she's sorry. She holds the door edge as he goes out, although she doesn't have to, there's no spring to pull it shut on him. She meant it as a gesture of politeness, but instead she feels like a gatekeeper, the person in control of who gets in, who stays out, who leaves with what information.

Opening

With the first sentence she puts on paper, Cath feels the mystery take hold of her. It's a current she hasn't created so much as floundered into by pure dumb luck.

"For the first half hour, Greg Sexton didn't worry," she writes. "He sat in the drivers' room with the new hires — the people who didn't have assigned cabs yet, the people whose names he hadn't bothered to learn.

"It wasn't like Greg's father to leave him waiting for the cab, but with Lyle there were always possibilities: a card game, a run to Duluth or Sleepy Eye that he hadn't bothered to call in, a bullshit session in an all-night diner taking his mind off everything but what was in front of him.

"Greg folded open the metro section of the paper. Flora Sexton — his dad's ex-wife, the woman he preferred not to think of as his mother — smiled out at him from page three. Her hair was overcurled and oversprayed, and her smile was inhumanly happy as she held two soft drinks toward the camera, one in each hand, demonstrating Greg had no idea what — something she thought would win her a vote or two.

"At seven he asked the dispatcher to call Lyle in. At seven-fifteen, he asked him to check whether anyone on the street had seen Lyle.

"'This isn't like him,' he said when the dispatcher hesitated. 'I'm getting worried here.'

"'Hey, this is Lyle we're talking about,' the dispatcher said. 'He could be anywhere.'

"'Humor me, okay? I'm worried about him.'"

Cath puts the pen down and breathes out. This is the first time she's believed the book is possible. It feels great. It scares her to the blood-rich core of her bones.

More Women

More women accumulate, but the pattern stays the same. Kara, for instance. She has a gorgeous laugh, and she shows up at the right time, and she isn't Megan or April, and Cath thinks how nice it is to have someone calling her, smiling when she sees her, sending notes that say "I miss you."

Within six weeks, she's ready to have Kara miss someone else. She's a perfectly nice woman, but Cath can't seem to breathe around her.

Then she meets Sasha. She's drawn to Sasha for who she is, not for who she isn't. A page turns. A chapter closes. This is it: the undiluted, hormonal loss of all critical faculties. Love. Cath goes home only to change clothes, water her plants, pick up her mail, and write. She drives back to Sasha's to sink into her bed, touch the smooth skin over Sasha's ribs, and breathe the air in her house, which tastes of sandalwood with a hint of German shepherd. They play the two-handed routines of domesticity as easily as if they'd always done them together. They cook, buy groceries, wash dishes, look through Friday's paper for a movie.

After her Swedish ivy dies, Cath bums two dry-cleaning bags from a neighbor, ties the tops, turns them upside down, and lowers her begonias into the tubes they form. She breathes the bags full of air and ties the open ends. This is supposed to protect them from the cold. It doesn't look like much in the way of protection, but Sasha works in her family's greenhouse and she swears it will work.

Cath warms the car up before she carries them out and at Sasha's she runs up the walk with one pot in each arm. It's February and somewhere between ten and twenty above. Once you get through a Minnesota January, this feels warm, but Cath hasn't explained that to the begonias.

Sasha takes a pot out of her hands as she comes up the stairs and shoves the door closed with a shoulder. The dog jumps at Cath, front paws in Cath's midsection. Cath raises the plant and yells, "No."

"Betsy, down," Sasha yells.

Betsy wags her tail. She doesn't get down until Cath brings a knee up underneath her, then she falls back and launches herself again, wagging her tail as wildly as if Sasha and Cath were cheering her on.

"Just poison her if you want to," Sasha says and turns her back on both of them. She sets the begonia she's holding on the coffee table. Cath tips the dog over again and follows Sasha.

"They okay?"

Sasha strips the plastic bag away from the first plant.

"They'll be fine. The car was warm?"

"As warm as it gets."

Cath peels her jacket off. She folds it over the arm of the couch to hang up later. Sasha's started picking through the first plant already, and watching her has the odd fascination of watching a chess match. She pulls off dead leaves and blossoms and piles them on the plastic bag.

Sasha's living room is so spare that if you tipped it the only things that would fall off the furniture would be a blue glass vase, a lacquered box, and dozens of glowing plants. Except for the dog, the only bits of disorder are Cath's fault.

When Sasha runs out of dead leaves, she begins pinching off live ones. Cath can't make herself object but does ask what Sasha's doing.

"It's good for it. It forces the growth to the base of the plant. Makes it grow fuller."

Betsy pushes her nose under Cath's hand and flips it to the top of her head to make Cath pet her. Cath pets, and Betsy puts a paw on Cath's knee. Her tail thumps the coffee table.

Sasha pulls the second plant in front of her and strips off the plastic.

"You shouldn't let them get like this."

"I water them. What more do they want?"

Sasha works automatically, like a musician practicing scales. She takes the question seriously and tells Cath how to water plants, and when, and what to pinch back, and which plants like what kind of light. Cath didn't want to know any of this, and if anyone but Sasha were saying it she'd take it as criticism. But it is Sasha, and Cath lets the information wash over her, happy to listen, not caring that she won't remember a word of it half an hour from now. Betsy lays her chin on Cath's knee, and when Cath stops petting her she tosses Cath's hand back to the top of her head.

"You're a worthless mutt," Cath says.

Betsy wags her tail. Sasha's fingers move through the begonia. The leaves look shinier already.

There's nothing in the world left to want.

Words like a Stone

Cath's father has bought a new handrail for the basement stairs, and it's lying across two sawhorses while he sits on a folding chair stroking blue paint onto the top and the closest side. He bends toward it from the hip, straight backed. It's an awkward way to work, and he paints slowly, methodically. He's never told Cath that his back hurts, but he walks slower these days, stiff and a little bowlegged, the way sailors walk, or the way they're supposed to walk. As far as Cath knows, she's never actually seen a sailor. She's seen bargemen on the Mississippi but only from shore when they pass. She has no idea how they walk.

If his back's bothering him, he shouldn't be in a damp basement. She thinks about saying this but can't imagine going upstairs into the summer heat any earlier than they have to.

A pair of ancient gooseneck lamps point down at the rail, and where the light strikes the paint it glows.

"How's that mystery of yours coming along?" he asks Cath.

Cath's been expecting this question. She'd be either relieved or hurt if he didn't ask. Whether she likes it or not, he's the reader she imagines when she sits down to write, and she's been telling him bits and pieces about her characters and plot since she began putting the story on paper.

Each time she does this, she swears it's the last time.

Cath shrugs. She's sitting on a high stool, elbows on her knees, on the opposite side of the rail.

"I haven't had much time—"

"Plot changed any?"

"Some."

He suspends the brush over the paint can, waiting for her to go on.

Cath pulls air into her lungs as if the whole story had to ride out on a single breath. This doesn't give her time to think of improvements, but it does leave time to look for them. She does this the way she'd look for a large, solid object she needed all of a sudden—an armchair, say, or a tire: She turns her mind in the direction of the story and hopes the improvements already exist.

They don't, and what she has looks shabby in the light of her father's gooseneck lamps. She says that the talk-show host has become a conservative, a born-again Christian. Her ex-husband, the cab driver, is a Jesse Jackson semi-Democrat, and he's been on the fringes of city politics for years. Every time the city council wants to expand the number of cab licenses or amend the cab ordinance, he gets drawn in. Just before he died, he tried to talk his ex-wife out of running for mayor. He thought she was dangerous—a charismatic candidate whose conscience is about as active as her appendix.

Cath's father dips the tip of his brush into the paint can and wipes it against the rim so the paint won't drip. He nods to her to go on.

"I tried to have her kill him herself, but it doesn't work. I think someone on her campaign staff will arrange to have it done—it'll be two steps away from her.

Her father says "Hmmh." He strokes paint onto the rail.

"You hate it," Cath says.

"Put a finger under there and hold this up why don't you. It'll save me painting the sawhorse."

Cath puts her fingers under the flattened side of the rail and holds it up.

"I like the idea of her turning conservative," she says as if he'd said he didn't. "It puts something more at stake. It feels like it's made the story bigger."

"Hold that steady."

Her father tips toward the rail. Through the wood Cath feels the stiff, even motion of the brush.

"So what's wrong with it?"

"Who said there's anything wrong with it?"

Cath waits.

"Go ahead and put that down. Be careful you don't get your fingers in the paint."

Cath sets the railing down and looks at her fingertips. Her father stands up.

"It's just that I don't see why you have to have someone else kill him. Why don't you let these people get their hands dirty?"

Cath brushes her fingertips against each other. It seems right to her that the people who pull the strings keep their hands clean. And that's part of the mystery—how to follow this particular string to its end.

"I don't know," she says. "I'll think about it."

Cath hasn't told her father that the co-owner of the cab — the person who unravels the murder — is now the son of the driver and the talk-show host. The son was peripheral the last time she mentioned him, and neither of them owned the cab.

Sometimes when Cath's not around her father, she imagines reading scenes to him. She imagines him liking them. She even brought the opening chapter to her parents' house once, but at the last minute she left it in the car. She hasn't read him any of what she's written, or let him read through it himself, and she never manages to tell him more than a few fragments before she shuts down, leaving what she hasn't said sitting inside her like a stone, trapped there as solidly as if there were magic in the world and only her father could say the words to knock it loose.

What he says instead is, "Come around here why don't you and hold up this end a minute."

She climbs off her stool and holds the unpainted end of the railing. The paint gleams under the gooseneck lamps like a landlocked Minnesotan's idea of ocean.

Beginning

Cath stands with her back to the phone and the metal-wrapped cord coiled snakelike over her arm. Across the airport concourse, Michelle's flipping through a rack of sweatshirts with the methodical distraction of a seasoned shopper. Tavi and Jean are out of town, celebrating their fifth anniversary, and Michelle spent last night at Cath's. This morning Cath's putting her on a plane to visit her grandparents.

The click of a machine answers Cath's call. Across the concourse, Michelle reaches the end of the sweatshirt rack and moves on to the magazines. When the machine reaches the end of its message, Cath turns toward the wall.

"Sash, pick up the phone if you're there." She waits while the tape on Sasha's machine winds from one reel to the other, recording the noises surrounding Cath— a businessman's voice on the next phone, a child's angry wail. "Sasha, we need to talk, damn it. Pick up the phone."

Her voice is too loud, and the businessman turns the expensive gray field of his back to her. He's talking to someone named Jeff, and his voice is upbeat and false.

Cath says "Sasha" and stops. She's been listening to the businessman and has lost the thread of her own conversation. Her nonconversation. She turns toward the empty phone on her left. A motorized cart beeps its way toward her, clearing a slow path ahead of itself. She lowers her voice.

"Look, if it's over, I can accept that, okay? But I've got to talk to you. You owe me that. Sasha, damn it, pick up the phone."

She waits again. A toddler lets go of her mother's hand and drops to the carpet, leading with her designer-covered diaper. The businessman beside her is quiet, listening to Jeff. Unless he's listening to Cath. To her own ear, Cath sounds like a high-school girl with a bad crush. Across the concourse, Michelle glances at a shelf of coffee mugs and paperweights with Minnesota motifs, then starts toward Cath. She's three years older than she seemed last year and wearing a letter jacket that's a size too big and a grade ahead of her. She's in eighth grade but swims on a high-school team. The jacket cost her a hundred and fifty dollars, and she had to gamble on growing into it but not outgrowing it. When Cath was that age, she was younger than Michelle seems. She was shy with adults and worried about what kids might think of her.

"I'll call you back," she tells Sasha's machine. "All I'm trying to do here is put this thing to rest so I can get on with my life."

The news that she isn't getting on with her life comes as a revelation to Cath, although once she hears the words, she can't think how she managed not to know it. She's spent the past two weeks talking to Sasha's answering machine. She's come up with a dozen reasons why Sasha hasn't called back, and she doesn't believe any of them. Last weekend she talked herself out of going to the laundromat so she wouldn't miss a call, in case one came. Her bathroom's dripping with half-dry underwear and shirts she rinsed out in the sink. The socks on her feet are yesterday's reruns. She hasn't written in weeks, hasn't gone out with friends, hasn't told anyone that Sasha's moved on, although Sasha's known for moving on—it won't surprise anyone once the word leaks out. It's been months since Cath's been able to finish a chapter, and before she stopped writing altogether, the bits she squeezed out were growing shorter and shorter. Somewhere on their way to the paper, her ideas were narrowing down until they disappeared completely.

She hangs up the phone, and Michelle comes up beside her.

"Hey, kid," Cath says. "You still got your ticket?"

Michelle unzips a compartment in her school bag and pulls up a corner of the ticket to show Cath, then pushes it back into hiding.

Cath nods behind her to the phone.

"You know, it's nuts how much energy people put into relationships. The world's falling apart around us and what do we think about? Why somebody won't pick up the phone."

"Who won't pick up the phone?"

Cath frowns.

"Sasha. You know Sasha?"

"The nervous one, with the dog. How come she won't talk to you?"

Cath shrugs. She'd have called Sasha intense, not nervous, but Michelle's probably right. They're walking toward the gate now, and neither of them is looking at the other. In the middle of the concourse, the bottom half of a man is visible, standing on a ladder. From the hips up, he disappears into an open space in the ceiling tiles.

"We split up," Cath says. "Or she split up. I guess I haven't yet."

Michelle doesn't say she's sorry to hear it. She doesn't ask why they split up or whether Cath isn't taking it all too hard. She lives in a parallel universe. She dips into Cath's from time to time, but only as an observer. She says "Oh," and her head swivels as they pass the jeans and the waffle-soled boots planted on the ladder.

Cath's asked herself both of the questions Michelle doesn't ask. She can't answer the first one. She suspects Sasha's met someone else, but Sasha hasn't actually told her yet that it's over. Cath answers the second question by referring herself to the first: She needs to hear the words. If Sasha would say what she has to say and get it over with, Cath could stop calling her the way she has been — six, eight, ten times a day. It's excessive. Cath knows that. It borders on harassment. Maybe it *is* harassment, but knowing the labels doesn't seem to help.

Before Michelle's interest can drift back to Sasha, Cath says she's been teaching a writing class through community ed. and tells her about the story one of her students wrote. It follows the panic of a woman waiting to board a plane. Inside her head, the woman hears an entire orchestra playing Mozart. Because Michelle's about to board a plane, Cath doesn't tell her that a few years before the story opens, the woman was on a plane, waiting to take off, when it was sliced open by the wing of another plane. She survived, but her faith in the odds didn't, and like Cath she's not getting on with her life. Cath lets the woman's fear sound like something she generates internally, the way her body generates liquids to digest her food and chemicals to carry her thoughts.

Cath's never talked to Michelle about writing before. She's mentioned River House, and they've talked about movies and fast food and television—the kinds of things she expects a kid to understand.

They find seats where they can see the jetway Michelle will walk through and the red-and-white tail fin of her plane. Michelle drops her school bag between her feet.

"Yeah, but how do you write a story?" she asks. "Like, say you've got an idea. How does it turn into a story?"

Beats me, Cath wants to say, both because she's less sure all the time and because she distrusts herself when she sounds authoritative. Teaching a class has reminded her of just how little she knows. But even more strongly she distrusts the impulse to make a joke right now—it would make Michelle's question sound foolish—so she asks for an example of an idea.

"Say you've got this girl who's afraid of dying," Michelle says.

On her neck Michelle carries a scar the size of Cath's hand, left from the time her birth mother burned her. This is the first year she's worn her hair short and let the scar show.

Cath asks what the girl's doing when she's afraid, and where she is, and they begin constructing a story. The girl's coming home after dark and is afraid a man will jump out of some hiding place to rape and kill her. The man isn't present; he's internally generated, like the fear of planes colliding on the ground. Cath supplies physical details: the sound of the girl's shoes on the sidewalk; the glint of the streetlight on a parked car where the man might or might not be hiding; the moment the girl stops to listen for him. She adds an argument between the girl and her mother, which leads the girl to storm out into the very dark she's afraid of.

Last night, Michelle told Cath about a boy in school who calls her Scarface. Every morning he looks at her and says, "Hey, Scarface." Once she asked him why he wanted to say something that hurtful to her. Another time she beat him up. He still calls her Scarface. Sometimes, she told Cath, it gets to her.

Over the public-address system a woman's voice calls the first-class passengers and anyone who needs extra time to walk down the jetway. Jumping over the gaps they've left in the story, Cath suggests an ending: The girl has to go home eventually. Suppose she goes to a friend's house and calls her mother from there. What's changed in her? she asks. What's changed between her and her mother? How much change would we believe?

"But what about the beginning?" Michelle asks.

"Once you have the middle and the end, how do you begin?"

The woman's voice calls the back rows. All around them, people assemble their carry-ons, their children, their jackets and coats. Cath talks about where the girl's argument with the mother starts and where the story could pick it up. It's rushed and arbitrary. She hears echoes of every bad beginning she's written herself. She can't hear a single good one. The woman calls the middle rows. At the entrance to the jetway, Michelle hugs her good-bye and says she'll write the story on the plane. She walks down the jetway without looking back. Cath stands looking after her until the last stragglers hurry onto the plane — a dozen of them, clustered together and rushing in from some connecting flight that landed late. Her eye's caught by a woman shepherding two girls in matching flowered dresses, their hair divided into a hundred tiny braids. There's just enough difference in their heights for them not to be twins. Not one of these people can know for certain that the plane will take off and land safely, but they move as casually as if they were pushing carts down a supermarket aisle. Somehow they've generated the courage to do this, even though planes can collide, mothers can set their daughters on fire, lovers can leave, and somewhere between the brain and the hand, the words to a story can become false. Most of them can afford not to know this, but Michelle begins every day with short hair and a boy waiting to call her Scarface.

Cath turns away and walks through the empty gate area, fingering the change in her pocket, automatically singling out quarters for the phone. She rubs one of them against another, then drops them back among the keys and dimes and pennies, telling herself, like a three-days-sober alcoholic walking past the liquor store, that she won't call from here, she won't call right now, although that doesn't keep her from eyeing the bank of phones ahead of her as if they could tell her what Sasha's doing at this exact minute. She's half a dozen steps past them when she stops, empties her pocket into an open hand, and picks through the change. She drops her keys and four pennies back into her pocket. The rest she pours into the coin-return slot of the last phone, and she leaves it there as an offering to the muse or a gift to the next caller, whichever one comes along first.

Other People's Sins

Holding the phone against her left ear, Cath spins her chair toward the office door and the goldfish bowl full of condoms that sits beside it. Last week, on Valentine's Day, she mixed in a handful of chocolates and waited for someone to notice. They'd disappeared by the time she got to work the next day, but no one's said a word about them.

She rests her feet on the open drawer at the bottom of the desk.

"Look," she says into the phone. "This isn't the kind of thing I can help."

She waits for Karen to say something. Karen doesn't, and when Cath can't hold out any longer she says, "Well, what am I supposed to do, tell Dallas to drag himself in to work anyway, sick or not sick, it isn't my problem?"

"There's other people that work there."

"Not that were available."

"See, there it is," Karen says. "That's what I mean. You weren't available either."

Cath lets air explode from her lips and break against the receiver.

"Not available as in didn't have day care, or as in

filled in for him last night. I'll come by tomorrow, for chrissake. I'll come by on Friday. That's the kind of job it is. It's not a thing I can change."

"It's not the job I'm talking about."

Cath brings her voice under control.

"Look, I'm sorry about tonight."

"It's not about tonight."

Cath spins to face the desk. She's staring at an outline of her head in the dark window, and beyond that at the orange streetlight. The temperature's been dropping all day, and the office is noticeably colder than it was this afternoon.

"So what is it about?"

Another pause while Karen decides whether to tell her. Across the street, a man's being pulled along the sidewalk by a dog. Cath sees the taut leash, the outstretched arm, the man's weight thrown backward to balance the dog's pull, but the dog itself is hidden behind a snowbank. Someone knocks on the office door, which Cath left open a crack to signal that she's available but would just as soon not be. Cath calls, "Come in," and tells Karen she'll have to call back, she shouldn't be long.

No one comes in. She calls out again and opens the door. One of the residents is waiting for her in the foyer, looking apologetic. His given name is Terrence, but everyone calls him Bill. He's in his early thirties — gay, black, good looking, very much this year's model. He's two months sober and only yesterday worked up the nerve to get a blood test. Now he's waiting to find out if he'll live a while. He apologizes for bothering her, but it's his turn to clean the third-floor bathroom, and he can't find any cleanser.

"I'd wait," he says, "but I've got a meeting at 7:30."

"Let me get my keys."

Bill follows her to the supply room and waits while she unlocks it. It makes sense to Cath that things are locked up, the world being what it is, but she feels like a jailer sometimes—the people come and go freely enough, but the things are under arrest. She wants to ask Bill when he'll hear about his test, but she can't do that outside the privacy of the office. Which might be why he waited for her in the foyer.

The supply room's more an oversized closet than a room, and everything's stacked against the walls, leaving a narrow path down the middle. She shifts a carton of lightbulbs, a small box of printer ribbons, and an industrial-sized case of toilet paper before she finds cleanser.

"Whatever happens," Bill says to her back, "I'm doing ninety meetings in ninety days. This'll be number two."

Cath hands him the cleanser and shifts the cartons back into place. These are AA meetings he's talking about. She has a hollow in her belly that feels like someone kicked a hole there, and she can't tell if it's about Bill's blood test or her phone call. None of the words she knows carry enough weight to be worth saying to him. Another AAer wouldn't have this problem. An AAer could say *One day at a time* if they couldn't think of anything else, and that would be enough—not because of the words themselves so much as what lies behind them.

Cath touches Bill's arm. She can do this with the gay men and not be misunderstood. He pats her hand as if she'd asked him for comfort and goes to clean the bathroom. Cath watches until he turns the corner of the stairs, then goes back to the office and leaves the door open a crack. The man with the dog is gone, and a car's idling in front of the apartment building across the street. She puts a hand on the phone and waits for some idea of what to say. What comes to mind is, *Listen, I just talked to somebody who may be dying, so what makes you think any of our problems matters?*

This is a great argument. The only thing wrong with it is that they do matter. Five weeks ago Cath slept with Sasha. She hadn't seen her in months and was surprised by how glad they were to run into each other. Sleeping together seemed like something they could both enjoy without hurting anyone—something that would put a better ending on their relationship. Karen still doesn't know about it, and Cath's been mad at her ever since. This makes no sense, but she can't seem to help it.

Cath dials without knowing what she'll say and starts by apologizing again—not for anything particular, just for life in general.

"I'll tell you what the problem is," Karen says.

Cath opens the center drawer and takes out a chain of safety pins that's been in the pen and pencil tray for as long as she's worked here.

"What?"

"What it is, is it isn't working."

Cath turns the tiny gold-colored pin at the end of the chain, first sideways, then lengthwise, then sideways again.

"It isn't," she repeats. She meant this to be a question, but it doesn't sound like one.

"I thought maybe we could work it out, but you're not even here."

Karen's voice breaks.

"I can't *help* that."

"You're not even here when you *are* here."

Cath folds the chain into her fist.

"I can come over tomorrow night."

"I'm sorry. I didn't want to do it this way."

A woman runs toward the waiting car, bareheaded and clutching an unbuttoned coat around her. It makes Cath cold to watch her.

"Would it have made any difference if I had come over?"

"I don't know." Karen's crying now. "I don't think so."

When Cath hangs up, she pulls a stack of forms in front of her and shuffles through them: residents' chart forms; vulnerable-adult assessment forms; care-plan forms; staff time sheets. She separates them into categories and evens the edges of each stack. It's some minutes before she realizes she hasn't done anything useful with them. She closes the bottom drawer with her foot, takes her keys, and locks the office behind her.

In the living room, one of the residents is sitting where he can watch the fireplace and the living-room doorway at the same time. Jack's in his late thirties and gives off a mixture of toughness and peace. He got sober in prison — the same place he got the tattoo between his thumb and index finger. Cath likes him. He doesn't change when he's with her. He doesn't try to say what she wants to hear.

Cath settles into a chair beside him, and they stare at the fire. In her head she replays the conversation with Karen. This time she tells Karen about Sasha. She explains that it wasn't something she planned — it just sort of happened to her, and it was wrong. She's sorry. All of this is true, but there's no force behind it, which makes Cath realize she doesn't want Karen to come back, she just doesn't want it to end this way.

Not that she has a better way in mind.

Jack stretches in his chair, settles back, and crosses his legs.

"Tutor didn't show up tonight?" she asks.

"Got the flu. Got a message from her this afternoon."

Jack's tutor is tall, perfect, beige. She's a volunteer for a literacy program, although Jack doesn't think of himself as illiterate. He reads well enough to fill out most forms: name, address, current employment. No one knew he had a problem until he marched into the office and announced that he'd been struggling with his pride and was ready to seek help. Jack talks like this sometimes — AAish, almost biblical. It gives him words for things he couldn't say otherwise.

The first time Jack met with his tutor, she told him she'd been trained by the literacy council. Jack stood up from the table where they were talking and walked out of the house. The tutor spent the next half hour in the office, crying and asking what she'd done wrong. It was two weeks before Jack could make himself meet with her again, and by then she had to be coaxed back.

The front door opens and shuts. Cold air laps at Cath's ankles. Jack calls out, "Liz?" then louder, "Hey, Lizzie?"

Liz clomps into the doorway and slumps there, all her weight on one leg, looking either awkward or sullen, depending on how you want to read it. Liz is twenty. She dyes her hair flat black and wears a hoop earring through her upper lip. On the side of her nose, just above the flare of her nostril, she wears a stud shaped like a fist with the middle finger raised. She has a collection of shapeless dresses and sweaters that she wears over white long johns and army boots.

"How'd it go?" Jack asks.

Liz opens her hand to show an AA medallion.

"You got it, hunh?"

She shrugs and says, "I guess."

"No guess about it. You worked harder for that than for anything else in your life."

The quick hint of a smile, and then a shrug.

"How many months?" Cath says.

Liz holds up three fingers like a kid telling someone how old she is.

"First three months are the hardest," Jack says.

Liz tips her head toward the staircase.

"I gotta go upstairs."

A log in the fireplace burns through and falls. Cath moves the screen aside and adds a new one. Liz's boots make a steady clump on the stairs.

"She was going to skip her meeting because of that medallion," Jack says when the clumping stops. "All those people looking at her. Made her nervous."

Cath sets the screen in place. Flames curl around the new log. She's impressed that Jack got Liz to go to her meeting. No one on staff has been able to reach her. Cath settles back into her chair, and the two of them stare at the fire like a long-married couple whose teenager actually came home on time, even if she isn't speaking to them.

"Jack?" Cath says after a while. "What are AA meetings like, if it's okay to ask. I mean, if that's not breaking the anonymity or anything."

"Depends where you go. People smoke a lot, talk about the steps — what they mean in their lives, how they understand them. Some meetings, people talk about what it was like when they drank, what they're doing to stay sober. Somebody has an anniversary, someone else gives them a medallion, talks about how they've changed, or what their sobriety's like. Doesn't sound like much when you talk about it, but it is."

The fire burns. In the dining room, someone calls, "Maxie, want to play hearts?" Three voices, then four. Laughter.

"It's the only thing kept me alive for a while there."

Jack taps a cigarette out of the package on the table between them, turns it in both hands, and fits it back into the pack. River House is smoke free. The smokers huddle on the front porch and stub their butts out in a tureen labeled NAVY BEAN SOUP.

"I made myself a promise back then —"

He taps the cigarette out, sets it between his lips, puts it back in the pack.

"Damn, I don't feel like going out in that cold."

In the dining room, someone deals out the cards. The fire sends up an explosion of sparks.

"What did you promise?"

"Doesn't matter. I got grandiose. You know drunks and junkies."

"So what'd you promise?"

Jack blushes. He's blond haired, light skinned. Cath's never seen him blush before. Somehow she thought he was immune to that. He lights up like neon.

"It'll sound dumb when I say it. I thought if I could ever keep someone else alive that way, through the program—. I don't know, maybe that's not a promise. I don't know what you call it. I figure I owe something, that's all. To whoever comes along."

He opens a book of matches, tears one off, tucks it behind the others, and turns the book in his hands.

"I told you it'd sound dumb."

Cath shakes her head and watches Jack's blush fade. In the next room, the card players laugh.

"I think you're a hell of a person."

"Then you don't know me."

Jack taps the same cigarette out and runs two fingers down its length.

"I look at myself in the mirror sometimes, I think, *Well, you're a miserable son of a bitch, but at least you're sober.*"

He puts the cigarette pack in his pocket and stands.

"I'll tell you one thing about a promise like that,

though. When you come down out of your grandiosity, it lets you know just how small you are in the world."

He looks at her for a few seconds as if he were measuring how small she is, then he heads for the entryway to get his jacket. Cath watches him until the wall cuts off her view. She hears the front door open, then close. Cold air laps around her ankles.

If Cath had met Jack when she was straight and not on staff here, she'd have jumped into bed with him, and they'd have had a brief, lousy relationship—on his side for a thousand possible reasons, on hers because she wouldn't have wanted either sex or love from it, she'd have wanted to annex some part of him for herself. She still does. The difference is that she doesn't have to sleep with him to know she can't have it.

She asks herself what part she wants, and the answer is, his pain. This is twisted, but she still wants it. She's convinced that her whole life would be clearer if she could join the fellowship of the wounded. In the dining room, Maxine's voice accuses one of the other card players of trying to shoot the moon.

"Look out for him," she shrills. "Don't give him *nothing.*"

Her voice is too high, too loud, too intense. Maxine will never pick up the signals that other people absorb by the time they're out of grade school. She'll always talk too loud, stand too close, get upset about the wrong things, and people will always back away from her, trying to get the distance right. No one will ever envy her pain.

Cath feels that boot in her belly again. She knows she's romanticizing AA. She doesn't want Jack's wasted years, or the years it will take him to put his life together. She doesn't want to live with his ghosts. All she wants is the strength that came from wrecking his life. She wants to confess someone else's sins and have people admire her honesty. She closes her eyes and leans her head against the chair. In the next room, Maxine shrills, and a man laughs and says, "My trick." Al, probably. A deep voice.

The ninth step tells AA members to make amends to the people they've hurt. If Cath were an alcoholic, she'd call Karen and confess. Then Karen would cry, and Cath would have caused pain without mending a damned thing. Her eyes are open again, and she's looking into the fire. She closes them and waits for Al to take the final trick, for Jack to come in from outside smelling of cold air and tobacco smoke, for Rosie to come at eleven so Cath can go home, for time to pass, and for what she's done to get smaller in the rearview mirror. She adds Karen to the list of things Cath has done wrong in her life. This does Karen no good at all, but it keeps Cath from believing the damage has been wasted.

Throwing Money Away

Two minutes before she'd meant to be out the door, Cath changes from shorts and a knit shirt to jeans and a shell, then from jeans into chinos. She puts on a necklace — a crystal on a leather thong, the kind that's supposed to purify your energy, or magnify your pores, or something along those lines. It makes her look like she's dressing up, which she emphatically is not; she's meeting someone for lunch, nothing more than that, and that someone only has half an hour. Cath checks her watch and hangs the necklace on the pegboard. She looks better without it. More natural. And she doesn't want Maggie to think she goes in for New Age hoo-rah. She turns back to the mirror to see if she's gotten any thinner, stronger, more graceful, or more likable. She hasn't, and she trades the shell for the knit shirt. It doesn't help, but she's more comfortable in it, and she's run out of time. She hangs up the clothes she threw on the bed and leaves without checking the mirror again.

Even with both car windows down, the back of her shirt's soaked by the time she parks. It's June. The air's as thick as cream soup. It practically ripples up in front of her as she pushes through it.

As soon as she's past the hospital's revolving door, the air's knife thin and cold. The speed of the door carries her half a dozen paces into the lobby, and she stops there and checks her watch. It's too early to go upstairs and too late to go home and start over. She's left with ten minutes to kill.

Lutheran's an old hospital, but the lobby Cath's standing in was grafted on recently, sometime after she quit driving cab. It's modern and ugly. The ceiling soars a good three stories above her head, and now that the initial pleasure of being cool is over, she's cold. The back of her shirt is clammy against her skin, and her body's nostalgic for the muggy air outside. She wraps her arms around herself.

A woman in a lab coat clacks past on hard-soled shoes, and a man carrying a child in one arm veers around Cath toward the door. She heads for the only welcoming place she sees, which is a gift shop, and spins the book rack by the door. It's stocked with crossword-puzzle books, bestsellers, inspirational stuff, books to take a person's mind off fear, sickness, pain. Nothing she wants to pick up and flip through. Nothing she wants to bring Maggie, but it makes her realize that she does want to bring Maggie something. Flowers, maybe. Balloons. Floating above the cash register is a clutch of mylar balloons, but they say, GET WELL, SORRY YOU'RE SICK, THINKING OF YOU. Cath is thinking of Maggie—she hasn't been able to stop thinking of her—but once the fact's printed on the face of a balloon it doesn't sound right.

The flowers are wrong too. They're offerings to the gods of health. Set them beside a bed, and death is supposed to turn away, reaching toward the body in the next bed. And flowers lead to questions. She's not sure Maggie's out at work, or how far.

In spite of which, Cath goes on looking at the flowers. Daisies, carnations, roses. She could be wrong about them. She's not good at this. She hates the idea of throwing money away on something that wilts in a few days, can't be eaten or worn, and whose only purpose is to say something Cath could say herself if she wanted to.

What she should have done is stopped on the way and bought a bouquet of peacock feathers — something expansive, outrageous, and with no known meaning in the language of love. She has no idea where she'd find such a thing, but that only makes the idea more appealing.

She thinks about candy, but what the store offers is all wrong — candy bars and megapackets of red licorice and lemon drops. It's a relief to have this choice closed off so clearly. Chocolate hearts would have made her uneasy.

Cath checks her watch and buys a plastic frog that walks sideways and waves its hands when she winds it up. In her pocket she carries directions: *north elevator to the seventh floor, turn right, you can't miss it.* She's written this last bit on the paper exactly the way Maggie said it this morning. It's not the kind of thing she usually writes down, but here it is, in her handwriting and Maggie's words, *You can't miss it.* She folds the paper back into her pocket. Her chest expands with the joy of breathing, and every fiber of her body believes that no, she can't miss it, all she has to do is turn right when she gets off the elevator, and Maggie will be there, cheering her on.

On the seventh floor, she turns right, and Maggie's sitting at the nurses' station wearing scrubs, her head bent over something Cath can't see but which must be paperwork — charts listing her patients' medications, breathing, blood pressure, other signals their bodies give off which Cath has no names for but which Maggie reads as easily as the letters of the alphabet. Her reading glasses ride low on her nose. She's a person you could trust with your life, with your windup plastic frog, with your chocolate heart, if you happened to have one. Cath stands still. She's seen squirrels freeze like this in front of oncoming cars, throwing split seconds away on the hope of invisibility before they bolt for a tree. Cath's too far gone to bolt, but she's grateful for this single moment before all thought drops away and she throws herself headfirst into Maggie's life.

Getting It Right

The day after her father's birthday, Cath brings over one of those cordless grass trimmers. She's taken it out of the box, assembled it, and tied a card to the handle, signed with her name and her brother's. Her father checks the card and hefts the trimmer, feeling its weight, its balance. He says, "Ha!" It's an approving noise. He likes the present. He likes that they went in on it together. He carries it into the living room so he can sit and admire it.

"Mary," he calls into the kitchen, "come look what the kids gave me. Al's been wanting one of these since last summer."

Al is their neighbor on the south side of the house, Cath's father's longtime friend and rival.

"I'll be there. Give me a minute."

"He'll drool. He'll hate me."

Cath beams.

"They're not quite as strong as the electric ones," she says.

"You don't let the grass get up to your knees, you don't need a lot of power. It'll be nice not to fight the cord all the time."

Cath agrees, but something in her wants to go on finding fault with it.

"Let me see if Mom needs help," she says.

"You know how she is in the kitchen. Sit down. Does it have an instruction sheet?"

It does, along with a warranty card, but Cath forgot them in the car, and she runs out to bring them inside. Her father reads everything printed on them: the instructions for changing the spool, the replacement spool's model number; if they printed it, he reads it. He asks questions she can't answer — the life of the battery, maintenance, whether it's better to keep it charged or leave it unplugged until the day before he needs it. She tells him where she bought it so he can call and talk to them himself. He heads for the phone, but Cath's mother starts bringing food out, and this isn't a call he's willing to rush.

Carrying food to the table is something Cath can safely help with. She brings in pot roast, butter, hot rolls, and her mother shifts each of them a fraction of an inch from where Cath set them down. Neither of them thinks to mention this.

"You do anything special yesterday?" Cath asks once they're sitting down.

"I tried to take your father out for dinner, but he wouldn't let me."

"And what's wrong if I wanted to take you out instead?"

Cath's mother gestures at him like she's annoyed, and he laughs. They're enjoying themselves. It's the way they flirt, this arguing. They've done it for as long as Cath remembers. She waits until they wind down and asks what they hear from Charlie lately.

156

The answer involves his new apartment—the lay-out, the neighborhood, the building. How Chicago's changed. Cath didn't think to ask about any of this when she talked to him, and he didn't mention it him-self. It's not something she cares about, but she can't help thinking she should.

After supper they watch an episode of *Mystery!* that her father taped. Cath has a hand on the doorknob be-fore he asks how her own mystery's coming.

"I'm working on it," she says.

"You got anything a person could read?"

Cath lets the doorknob go, and her hand reaches into her pocket. Automatically, it starts fishing for her keys.

"It's an early draft still. It needs too much work."

"I'd like to see it all the same."

"It's pretty much of a mess, Dad."

They nod, assuring each other of their goodwill, their agreement, their mutual understanding.

"As soon as I get it right," she says.

"I want to be the first one to see it, you hear?"

She says that's fair enough and puts her hand back on the doorknob. She wonders if this will freeze her writing again and decides neither of them really means what they said. They were being polite. They nod at each other some more, and she lets herself out into the warm summer night.

Atoms, Molecules

Sitting in bed beside Cath, Maggie explains it this way: She and Paul made promises to each other when they split up, and she's not going to be the first one to break them. They promised to respect each other's rights as parents; they promised that when Trina was old enough to understand they'd explain that they'd been married once and were still friends; they'd tell her they both loved her; however mad they got at each other, and no matter who else they got involved with, they'd never fight through her. So it's important that Cath and Paul meet and everything be out in the open.

Cath nods. Maggie's fingers are playing with her hair and touching her scalp. Cath's lying on her back, staring into the mirror above the dresser, where she sees the wall behind their heads and half a dozen turn-of-the-century photographs of people Maggie knows nothing about except that their descendants got rid of their pictures, either because they'd forgotten who the people were or because they wished they could. Maggie's gallery of adult orphans, unsmiling and proud, holding themselves straight for the photographer with rigid, antique grace.

Maggie's grace is of a different sort than the orphans'. It comes from fluidity, and from a belief that whatever she's wearing and no matter how ratty it is, it looks great on her. What she's wearing right now is a worn black tee shirt she bought at a garage sale last weekend. It has a red rose and the name of a bar above the left breast. Above the hem it has a cluster of small holes. It looks great.

"So how well do they work?" Cath asks, meaning the promises.

"Pretty well, considering." The top of Maggie's head rests a few inches below the lowest picture, and Cath wonders fleetingly what these strangers would think of the use their images have been turned to. "He's a decent person. The problem is that when you have kids, you never get to divorce each other all the way. You keep having to come back and try it one more time with someone you already know you don't get along with. Still, if I've got to be not quite tied to somebody, he's the one I'd choose. I don't know, if he was a woman I'd probably still be with him."

Cath nods. She and Maggie have been seeing each other for a couple of months and already they've talked about living together. Or they've started to talk about it. They always end up talking about how it would affect Trina. Cath practices thinking of herself as a parent, as a stepmother, as a kind of distant adult roommate. It scares the hell out of her.

"What if I send him a card or something and go home first thing in the morning?"

Maggie reaches under the sheet and pinches her — not a mean pinch, just enough to register an opinion.

"Okay, a card *and* a present."

Maggie pinches again.

"It's too weird," Cath says. "It's like meeting your date's parents when you're in high school, only weirder."

Maggie slides down beside Cath and puts a hand on her arm, fingertips reaching just under the hem of her sleeve. She has a look on her face that means she's not going to let go of this, and she says please, it's important to her. Cath looks at the strangers on the wall behind their heads; her mind is tracking the course of Maggie's fingertips on her arm.

"All right, I'll do it, but it's weird."

Maggie's fingers reach farther up toward her shoulder. Cath rolls onto her side, pulling her arm away. She makes a mental list of the reasons to live alone. It includes finding her shoes where she left them, without any Legos stuffed in the toes. This is petty, but she leaves it on the list anyway.

Cath doesn't meet Paul until early Sunday evening, when he brings Trina home. He's a small man wearing cutoff jeans and sandals. He shakes hands with Cath and accepts the beer Maggie offers. He sprawls at the end of Maggie's couch and taps the beer unevenly against one bony knee. Trina's tiny plastic suitcase nestles against his leg. Somehow he's started talking about his fish tank — Cath can't reconstruct how or why he started talking about this, but suddenly here he is, in the middle of algae and pH levels and the territoriality of different species. He's lost a lot of fish lately, and he runs through all the reasons why this might be happening. He's either very knowledgeable or he's one of those men who makes a little information stretch a long way. Cath's not really listening, but she's grateful to him for filling the silence.

Cath is at the opposite end of the couch from Paul, and her eyes are on Trina, who's sitting halfway up the stairs, tracing the banister posts with one finger, taking in whatever it is that she takes in, and saying nothing. She's wearing a knit shirt that's three sizes too big. The neck's wide enough for her own head and several other people's to pass through at the same time. She draws her knees up and stretches the shirt over them. Sitting here with both her parents, she's quieter than Cath has seen her before. Maybe she's afraid to favor one of them over the other, or maybe she's a different person with each of them and doesn't know who to be when they're together. Maybe she suspects there's more to their story than she's been told, and she's trying to read the secret history of her existence in the lines of their bodies and the pitch and mix of their voices. On the other hand, her quietness may have nothing to do with them; she may be trying to figure out how Cath fits into the family.

Maggie explained Cath to Trina once. She said Cath was Mommy's friend, and that Mommy loved her. Cath's not used to the number of things that have to be explained to kids, and she was terrified that Maggie was going to use the word *lover*. Eyeball-to-eyeball with a five-year-old, *lover* sounds a lot more graphic than it does in normal conversation. Trina didn't ask any questions about Cath's role in her life. She didn't argue, she didn't complain, and she didn't look like she was listening. What she did do was tear open the velcro straps on her sneakers and close them again, tear them open and close them, so that anytime Cath thinks about moving in with Maggie and Trina, she hears the sound of velcro ripping.

Maggie has sunk into the brown velvet armchair by the door. This is an old chair, worn smooth on the arms and sprung in the seat but elegant in its broken-down way. She's nodding and making wordless I'm-listening noises while Paul talks. This convinces Cath that Maggie isn't listening either. When Paul stops talking and takes a swallow of beer, Maggie looks intently into the open tab of her own beer, which she's been rolling back and forth in her hands and not drinking. When Paul lowers his can, he looks half panicked, as if he's run out of information and can't remember what else people talk about. Maggie studies her beer. Trina walks her fingers up the banister post.

"About next weekend," he says finally. He taps the beer against his knee. "You have any plans for Friday night?" He swings his eyes to the left almost enough to include Cath in the question, then they snap back to Maggie. He looks sheepish. "I mean that couldn't, you know —"

He gestures vaguely with his free hand to fill in the blank space, then laughs at his awkwardness.

"You want to pick her up Saturday morning?"

He snaps his fingers and points at Maggie. "Bingo! We have a winner!"

Maggie smiles. Cath has the feeling she's watching their entire marriage condensed to a five-second film clip. Then Maggie turns to her to see if she'd counted on the two of them having Friday night to themselves. Cath shrugs. She's counted on nothing, but even if she had, her wants are stuck in neutral right now.

"It's all tentative," Paul says. "It's nothing I couldn't—" He shrugs helplessly, shakes his head, and mimes slitting his wrist, drawing the line upward, along the artery instead of across, the way you cut if you want to die, not just bleed. He laughs. "God, it's like asking for a date when you're thirteen."

Maggie laughs. If she attaches any meaning to his gesture, she doesn't show it.

"Saturday's fine." She looks over her shoulder. "That okay with you, Treen? If Daddy picks you up Saturday morning?"

Trina nods. Her finger runs up the banister post, circles one of its indentations, and runs down. She's too young still to understand what slitting your wrists means, but Cath's shocked that Paul would do this in front of her. You can't predict what a child will store away and make sense of later. Cath stores it away under Bad Parent in case she needs it. She doesn't ask herself what she might need it for.

Paul is smiling like a man who's been pardoned for all his sins, past, present, and future. He wouldn't have shocked Cath if he'd made the usual slit-your-wrists gesture, the crossways one that amateurs use.

"I should go, then," he says. He tosses back a last

swallow of beer and stands. Maggie stands. Cath stands. She jams her hands into her pockets and says she's glad to have met him.

"Likewise," he says. "I'm sure we'll—"

He gestures vaguely, gives up, and crosses to the stairs to make a monkey face at Trina, scratching his ribs. He looks easy doing this. He straightens and says, "See you next week, short stuff."

Trina waves her fingers at him and bites her upper lip in a half monkey face that's meant to be visible only to him.

Maggie walks Paul to the front porch.

"Around ten?" he says.

"Ten's fine."

They nod at each other a couple of times.

"Ten o'clock, then."

Paul opens the screen door a couple of inches and says thanks, he appreciates it, it's just that—. They nod some more. They smile and shrug.

Paul and Maggie have been separated for three years and divorced for two. They still haven't figured out how to say good-bye to each other. The flies rush in and out. Maggie says it's fine about next weekend, it's no problem, it's not a competition. He says he appreciates it. Finally he sets his feet on the front steps and holds the door open from there. Cath marches herself to the couch and sits down, still listening for the swat of door against frame.

Finally Maggie comes back in, swings Trina's tiny suitcase into the air, and sweeps Trina upstairs to help unpack it. She's upbeat, efficient, admirable. Cath's not sure what to do with herself. She stretches out and leafs through the TV guide, listening to their voices. This is one of the things being a parent means: You don't say what's on your mind until the kid's in bed, or playing in another room, or busy with a friend, and by then it's not a thought or a feeling, just the fossilized remains. It's been replaced cell by cell until it has the same shape but the texture and makeup are completely different.

And for all you know the kid overhears you anyway.

When they come back down, Trina's dangling her Barbie doll by the hair. The doll's name is Ashley. All Trina's dolls are named Ashley. Trina settles into the velvet armchair and runs a red felt-tip pen more or less across the doll's lips.

"She's going out," she tells Cath.

Cath sits up and nods soberly. The ghosts of a thousand ancestors whisper and hiss inside her head—the mothers and the grandmothers, hers and Maggie's and those of women she's never met, all of them telling her to stop the child, she's being bad, and for her own good, she needs to know this.

"She can't go out without lipstick?" Maggie asks.

"She likes lipstick."

Maggie rocks her head from side to side in a motion that doesn't so much disagree as withhold agreement. A siren screams past the house and stops down the block. Trina's head turns to follow it, and the hand with the pen arcs in slow motion toward the arm of the chair. Cath dives for it, lifts it back into the air, and takes the pen. She says, "Be careful," and wants her voice to have been neutral instead of tight, which is how it came out, but even so the grandmothers are howling that she hasn't said enough. The child is careless. She needs to be told this. How else do children learn?

Does this chorus mean that Cath doesn't like Trina, or doesn't like the way Maggie's raising her, or doesn't like kids in general? Does it mean her mother will take over all her dealings with children, so maybe she shouldn't have any? The questions are important, and she doesn't have answers for them. Another siren goes past. Trina leaves the doll on the chair and runs to the porch, yelling back that they're fire engines and she wants to go watch them. Maggie tells her to come put the cap on the pen first.

A few seconds creep past in silence.

"It doesn't have one."

"It had one when you found it, so go look for it."

Trina plants herself in the doorway and stamps. She tries to produce tears, and when she can't she whines. Maggie keeps her voice even. She explains about felt-tip pens and ink drying out. She suggests places for Trina to look. The grandmothers howl. Finally Trina drags herself up the stairs, the toes of her red sneakers scraping on the rim of each step.

"It's not here," she yells as soon as her feet touch the upstairs hall.

"Keep looking."

Trina thumps and rattles.

"He's a decent guy," Maggie says as if they'd just been talking about Paul.

"He seems nice," Cath says. "A little uncomfortable, maybe."

Maggie laughs.

"He must have a date." She's whispering, her head cocked toward the stairs to listen for Trina. "Good news is the only thing that would make him that awkward."

Cath remembers his empty hand slicing upward along his arm.

"I thought maybe it was me," she says.

"Maybe that too. A little."

"Mom," Trina wails, "I can't find it."

"Look where you found the pen."

"I di-id."

"Then look again."

"I can't."

"Katrina."

A thump on the ceiling.

"When I think about what some women go through," Maggie says, talking about Paul again. "Courts and lawyers and ex-husbands kidnapping their kids."

"You don't worry?" Cath nods toward the stairs, and Maggie shakes her head, no. They're talking about custody: Is Paul the sort of man to sue for custody now that he knows about Cath?

"He's not like that."

Cath wants to ask how she can know, but Trina comes downstairs, arms folded, her whole body radiating sulk. She hands the top of a pen to Maggie and waits to see what will happen. The top is black. Cath wonders how bad it could be if Paul did win custody, and a wave of guilt swarms through her.

Maggie caps the pen without comment.

"Let's go see about those fire engines."

Trina's arms tighten around her body.

"I don't want to."

Maggie closes her eyes for a second, sighs, and picks Trina up. Trina holds herself stiff, like a giant Barbie doll, all rigid plastic, and lets herself be hauled out to the front walk. Cath stops to lock the door behind them. The sun has just set, and the evening feels soft and endless. Somewhere upstairs the ink inside a black pen is turning to dust. The grandmothers have pretty well given up on Cath, but they whisper that she could at least go back and put the red cap on it. They shake their heads and frown. They don't approve of waste.

Maggie sets Trina down, kneels, and puts her hands on Trina's shoulders while Trina looks away, head turned tight over one shoulder, doing her best to disappear. Cath walks past them to the sidewalk and waits, but even from here she can hear Maggie's voice — not scolding but somehow harder to take than if it were. She turns away to give them all some privacy.

Maggie's neighborhood is made up of small, neat houses, most of them built in the twenties. She claims that because she's single the neighbors on both sides worry that she won't mow her lawn or shovel her walk, and if they get to their lawn mowers or their snow blowers before she does, they march on over and take care of her yard and sidewalk for her. She's never sure whether to thank them or run them off her property. It's true that the lawns on both sides are neater than

Maggie's—carefully edged and free of weeds—but their flowers are spindly things, all lined up in single file, as neat as soldiers. Maggie's are thick, disorganized, and luxuriant. The neighbors probably disapprove of them.

Maggie joins Cath and they stand together quietly for a few seconds. Both the fire trucks and the fire are out of sight, but a police car's parked crossways at the corner, blocking traffic, and they begin walking toward this, Cath and Maggie in front, Trina dragging herself behind, scraping her feet against the sidewalk.

"Must be a garage," Cath says.

"Makes sense."

Trina's far enough behind that they could hold an adult conversation, and Cath searches for something she's been wanting to say, but nothing more than this is ready for words. If Trina didn't exist, she'd still say, "Must be a garage," and Maggie would still say, "Makes sense." If the world were different, she might put an arm around Maggie's shoulders to see if it would pull them closer to each other, but that has nothing to do with Trina.

Cath nods backward.

"She okay?"

Maggie shrugs.

"She's got a temper, doesn't she? She'll be all right."

They find a fire truck near the alley, and fire fighters folding their hoses back into it. The front and side of the nearest garage are heavily burned. Half the neighborhood has turned out to watch, but they're beginning to leave now. First a pack of kids rides off on bikes, as sudden as a flight of starlings, then a few of the adults, in ones and twos, drift back to their televisions and their dinner dishes, moving as slowly as the late-summer dusk. Maggie introduces Cath to a stout, thirtyish woman with brown-blond hair and a voice that's twenty years too young for her. Trina pushes past them, still angry, and stops in the front rank of specta-tors. The neighbor's telling Maggie about the garage — about the ex-girlfriend of the son of the family that owns it and how she's been calling the boy up, threat-ening one thing and another, but no one took her seri-ously until now, and when you think what could have happened if she'd chosen the house instead —. The neighbor's face disapproves, but her voice is vibrant.

When Cath turns to look at the ex-girlfriend's handiwork, Trina's moved a few steps forward and is standing alone between the adults and the garage. Be-fore Cath can turn away, Trina moves forward another step and freezes there.

When Cath was eight or ten, her brother told her that if she moved slowly enough she'd look like she was standing still. Cath didn't quite believe him but wasn't sure enough to call him a liar. Someone must have told Trina the same thing, and watching her creep forward — step-freeze, step-freeze — Cath feels an odd mix of triumph that she was right and pain that Trina's let herself be taken in. Cath turns away so her interest won't make Maggie notice Trina and call her back. When she lets herself look again, Trina's almost at the garage. Her pauses are shorter and her steps longer. Maggie's neighbor has started telling stories about another neighbor, someone Cath doesn't know, whose burnt garage she hasn't stood staring at.

When Trina's within arm's length of the garage, she lays the flat of her hand on its charred wall and rubs it back and forth. The front rank of adults, Trina's screen, says its good-byes and drifts off. Cath walks up the soaked driveway and stands beside Trina.

"Ever seen a fire before?"

Trina shakes her head without looking around. She lifts her hand away and begins a motion that will end by wiping it clean on her shirt. Cath's mouth opens, but the words don't become sound until Trina's swiped her hand from shoulder to rib, leaving a streak of charcoal behind. Cath says, "Don't," and then, "Never mind," and closes her mouth. Trina turns to face her. She's not a bad-looking child, but she's not pretty either, and Cath runs a hand over the back of Trina's head, wishing she could protect her against the people who will sooner or later make her feel not-pretty. Trina's shirt has slipped to one side, and her shoulder pokes through at the neck, as insubstantial as a bird's wing. She smells of fire, of wet ash, of living matter's vulnerability to sudden and unwilled change. Even now her bones are growing heavier, longer—growing so slowly that no one can see it happen. If neither fire nor her father snatches her away, time will, changing her in ways Cath can't predict but feels as a loss.

Cath nods at the charred wood.

"You understand how this happens?" she asks.

"It burnt."

"Yeah, but do you know why it leaves the wood like this?"

Trina shrugs.

"It has to do with atoms," Cath says, "and molecules. See, the fire needs oxygen to burn —"

She stops herself. She was on the point of saying that fire drives oxygen molecules out of the wood so it can burn, and that this is what changes it. As far as she knows, this is complete nonsense — she has no idea why she was going to say it. Trina's looking at the blackened wood. She may be listening, and she may not be.

"You want to know the truth," Cath says, "I don't know why it turns black. It's just what fire does."

Trina nods — this is no more than she expected, and no less. They turn back toward Maggie, and Trina takes hold of Cath's hand as if this were the most natural thing in the world. The streetlights blink on, pale orange against the blue twilight and almost too faint to notice.

Distant Touch

Cath sits in a hospital coffee shop watching a woman in scrubs walk toward her. The woman's blond and athletic looking, and she knows she's being watched. Her face goes blank, and her eyes fasten on some spot beyond Cath, at the far end of the room. Cath looks away, but a second later she's watching the woman walk again. She needs the motion. She needs a steady flow of people to keep her from joining one thought fragment to the next, from connecting *My father's dying* to whatever would naturally follow that.

Sooner or later a thought will have to follow, but Cath's in no hurry to find out what it is. It's enough to know that she'll remember sitting in this place long after she's forgotten more important things. She'll remember the off white of the walls and the sixtyish couple sharing a sweet roll at the next table. The woman pulls tiny pieces off the roll, eating some of them herself, urging some of them on the man, and he accepts them gently, almost reluctantly. Birds court like this, or a few species do — goldfinches, cardinals, canaries. With birds, though, the male does the feeding. The people are stout and mild featured, and Cath tries to imagine the person they've been sitting with upstairs, but she can't connect them with another person, only with each other, with this moment, with how fondly she'll remember them long into the future.

She'll remember her brother less fondly but also just the way he is right now, coming toward her with a plastic tray in his hands, and on the tray two styrofoam cups and two sweet rolls in cellophane bags. He's filled out since she saw him last — or else he filled out years ago, but she's gone on seeing him the way he used to be. His face has the look of someone who once thought hard work and initiative would take him somewhere and who now thinks he was a damn fool. Charlie sells sports equipment, and he's stalled out somewhere below the suit-wearing level. It's been years since Cath felt comfortable asking about his job, and even longer since he talked about it without being asked.

He sets his tray down and unloads their coffee, along with a handful of plastic cream containers and packets of sugar — more of them than any two people could use. Charlie's heard of finite resources and wants to make sure he gets his share.

He pulls out the chair across from her and sits.

"So the doctor doesn't expect much," he says, not asking as much as tossing out a statement to see if she'll argue.

"He kept using the word *massive*," she says. "Massive damage. Massive this, massive that." She runs one finger around the lid of her coffee cup. "He didn't want to do any more than make him comfortable. It was Mom—"

Cath waits for Charlie to pick this up, but he doesn't. He's seen the tubes and monitors and machines that anchor their father to his life. He doesn't want to hear how they got there. He says, "I've been thinking about Mom."

Cath nods. Their mother's upstairs, waiting for the nurses to let her back into their father's room. She told Cath and Charlie to walk around, to get some coffee, to not feel like they have to sit with her every minute, and they left together as meekly as kids who are old enough to behave well in a strange place but not old enough to know what they should do there unless someone tells them.

Charlie pries the lid off his coffee.

"The question is, what's going to happen to her afterward?"

Cath opens a container of cream and pours it into her coffee. She pushes the foil cover into the container, sets it down, and picks up a plastic stir stick. Even with these, Charlie's taken more than they need. They lie on the tray like a Rorschach test. *I see excess, doctor. I see waste. Is that within normal parameters?* She flexes the stick between her hands. She should nod here, or say *Yes?* or dig her heels in and argue with she's not sure what yet. Instead she puts the plastic stick into her coffee and stirs. On the other side of the aisle, a man sweeps a table clear of empty sugar packets and styrofoam cups, then sprays the table down and wipes it.

"The house is going to be too much for her. It's not just the yard and the snow, but maintenance, repairs—" Charlie nods his head to the side as if the list is much longer but too obvious to need spelling out.

Cath shakes her head. She takes the stir stick out of

the cup, and the coffee goes on circling without her help.

"What's that mean?" he asks.

"It's too early to think about it."

"We've got to think about it." His voice is solid, responsible. He wants to take care of their mother. Cath's being sentimental. "You're not going to show up every Sunday and mow the grass, are you? You're not going to reroof the house."

"You're not going to reroof it either."

"Exactly."

"Dad wasn't going to reroof it."

"That's not the point."

"It doesn't *need* reroofing."

Charlie pinches the skin above each knuckle methodically. This is their father's gesture. Cath can't remember whether Charlie's always done it or whether he's moving into the space their father hasn't quite moved out of yet. She looks away to keep from snapping at him. The couple at the next table have finished their sweet roll and are talking slowly and quietly to each other—a few words, an easy silence for the words to land in, a few more words.

"You're not listening to what I'm saying," Charlie says. "An old house always needs something—the roof, the painting, the plumbing. You know how to snake out a drain or rewire a light fixture? If it isn't one thing, it's another. All I'm telling you is it'll be more than she can keep up with."

Cath runs her fingers through her hair.

"I'm not having this conversation, okay? Nobody's dead yet."

Charlie makes a disgusted sound, pours two containers of cream into his coffee, and stacks the empties inside each other, then inside the container she's emptied.

"You're not being realistic."

Cath's braced for him to say more, but he's not being realistic either. He doesn't want to talk about what's coming any more than she does. They look away from each other. Cath thinks how odd it is that they're not crying, but there isn't a tear in her, and she can't imagine where one would come from. All she can imagine is what's right in front of her: the white top of the table, their hands and coffee cups, this dry bone of a woman, her even drier brother.

She breaks her sweet roll out of its body bag. It's almost square, with squiggles of icing across the top. The thought comes to her, fully formed and in words, that if she were anywhere else in the world she wouldn't eat this. She breaks off a corner and chews. It tastes of sugar, of oil, of something long ago descended from apple.

"When do you have to be back at work?" she asks.

He hesitates before he answers—just long enough that she can hear him decide not to argue.

"I'll call on Monday and see what I can negotiate."

It's not until they're on the elevator and he's punching buttons for the sixth floor, and for the door to close right away, without waiting for anyone else, that she thinks of what she should have said: that she doesn't want to make plans for their mother unless their mother's part of the discussion; that it isn't up to them to decide for her. For a second she wonders who she might have been if Charlie hadn't been in her life from the moment she was born, always placing himself next to the elevator buttons, the TV controls, the levers that choose the time, place, and subject of every conversation.

Their mother's not in the waiting room when they get upstairs, and Cath calls the intensive-care desk to ask if she can see her father. The rules allow two visitors for twenty minutes of every hour, but when she and Charlie walk past the desk together no one looks up to count heads, add their mother's, and come up with a total of three.

Their mother's head is nodding, but she raises it automatically when they get close to the door. After all these years, she's still tuned to the vibrations of their shoes on the floor.

"I must've been asleep," she says, but already she's shaken off any trace of haziness. She's as alert as Cath's ever seen her—a guard dog disguised as a sixty-seven-year-old woman. She'd snap death himself in half if she could get her jaws around him. It's the role she's been training for all her life. She'd be the same way if Charlie needed her. Or if Cath did. She'd tear them away from carjackers, cops, drug-crazed Hell's Angels armed with assault weapons. She's never had a crisis worthy of her till now.

Cath holds out the sweet roll and coffee they brought. Their mother didn't ask for anything, but it seemed important to bring something back, even if it was only this—food you eat not because you want it but because you don't know what else to do, and because you remember, in an abstract sort of way, that the living have to eat.

"Did you bring sugar?"

Cath nods at the cup.

"It's in there."

"Good girl."

Something catches in Cath's throat. A host of green lights draw lines on the monitor above her father's bed. A machine forces air into his lungs. Her mother takes the lid off her coffee and sets it on the bedside table to cool. She won't drink it until it's almost cold, when it holds just the faintest memory of heat. She toys with the wrapper on the sweet roll.

"I could get you a sandwich instead," Cath says.

"I can't even think about food."

Cath nods as if she understands, although in fact she could eat again right now, without hunger and without end. The taste of apple and sugar lines her mouth, and she wants something to replace it—tunafish; a hamburger with pickles and ketchup; a ham sandwich with mustard. She's standing by the head of her father's bed. Tubes disappear into his mouth. The thick one is air; the green one, food. Each time the pump forces air through him, his chest bucks under the blanket like he's trying to push it back out. With each breath, the machine ticks, then sighs. Cath touches his forehead with two fingers. In the next glass-walled room, liquid gurgles inside a tube, making a sound like a kid sucking the last drops of Coke through a straw, only thicker.

"We're all here, Dad. Charlie's here. Mom's here."

She wants to say her own name but can't. The machine forces air into his lungs. At the nurses' station, a phone rings. Cath tries to believe that her father hears her, but she doesn't quite. He's sedated heavily, and there's no telling how much damage the heart attack did to his brain. Still, she wonders if there's anything she wants to tell him—any last message to shoot after him into the void. If she were alone with him, she'd read him what she has of the mystery, never mind how raw and unfinished it is. She'd tell him what the talk-show host is hiding in her past: someone's death. What else is there to hide from? It was kind of self-defense and kind of an accident, and the talk-show host doesn't want to try and prove either of those statements in court.

Cath doesn't tell him this, but she hates the idea of him sliding out of the world without having seen that she really is putting words on the page, and with nothing to listen to but the tick-sigh of an electronic metronome.

"Charlie," their mother says, "go see if you can find your sister a chair."

"I'm okay, Mom. I'm fine."

Charlie's been leaning against the doorway, and he pushes himself upright, waiting for them to make up their minds. Their mother nods at him and says, "Go."

"Mom—" Cath says.

"It won't hurt to let someone do something for you once."

"I should go home anyway. I need a shower."

Cath's mother softens visibly.

"What kind of mother am I anyway? Of course you should go."

This is an old family joke—what kind of mother am I anyway?—and Cath smiles. She notices that she can do this, and it strikes her as overwhelmingly odd that she's smiling at a joke she always hated while her father lies beside her, dying.

"I could drive you home if you want to change or something."

"Later. Maybe after visiting hours."

Cath's father and his machine breathe in unison. Charlie lumbers back with a chair and sets it beside their mother's.

"I'm going home in a minute," Cath says. "I'm too grubby to be out in public."

Charlie shrugs—he's not responsible for his sister's whims. She wants to remind him that she spent last night in the waiting room with their mother, curled up on the floor with her jacket bunched under her head, only Charlie knows this already. He spent most of last night driving up from Chicago, finally stopping to grab some sleep when he realized that the lightning he was seeing had nothing to do with the snow clouds and everything to do with exhaustion.

Cath touches her father's forehead again. His skin's oily. Maybe it always has been. She can't remember touching his forehead before today, although she must have when she was little.

"I'm going home for a few minutes, then I'll be back," she tells him.

The machine breathes. He resists.

"I won't be long," she tells her mother.

"We'll be fine."

Cath touches her mother's shoulder. On her way past Charlie, she touches his arm, and he pushes away from the doorway and says he'll walk her out.

At the nursing station, a man's telling two women something so full of medical language that all Cath understands are the pronouns and prepositions—*I, out, you, him, off.* Along the wall someone's parked a tank of compressed gas and a pair of machines with dials all over them. Everything's on wheels, as if the whole unit's made to be rolled away. All they're waiting for is some financial wizard to decide they can make more money from a cafeteria, or a theme park.

"I'm glad you were with her last night," Charlie says when they reach the elevators.

He sounds unsure. He's not used to saying this sort of thing and can't tell if he has the accent or the order of the words right.

Cath glances down, nods, shrugs.

"How do you think she's doing?"

"I'm not sure any of us know how we're doing right now."

He laughs, not because she's funny but by way of agreement. She touches his arm again and says she really should go.

Outside, the sun's blinding and there's fresh snow on the ground. When she drove to the hospital last night, she watched this same snow falling. She's as fond of it as she is of the couple in the cafeteria. It floated down gently, almost weightlessly. About two inches, all told. The radio had predicted four.

A cab pulls up in front of the hospital door, and the driver hauls himself out like every bone in his body is tired. Cath doesn't know him, but she stops to watch him walk inside. More than anything else she can think of right now, she wants to be that driver.

Didn't Sam warn her this would happen?

She calls Maggie from her apartment. In the background, a woman's voice is paging someone. Maggie works at Lutheran, and Cath's father was taken to Riverside, but the voice is the same one she's been hearing all morning—soothing, bland, letting everyone know the situation's under control, there's nothing to get upset about.

Maggie asks about medications, about the oxygen level in Cath's father's blood, and Cath says she's not sure, she doesn't know, she didn't ask. She remembers a doctor leaning against the wall to talk to her and her mother. She remembers the metal frames on his glasses, a single white hair growing wild out of his black eyebrows. She remembers knowing that her mind was reaching overload. All she really understood was that her father was dying. She remembers her mother saying she didn't give a damn about the odds, she wanted him to have every chance, as if there were still chances to be had.

"I'll stop by as soon as I get off work," Maggie says.

"Mag, my uncle's coming by, we're in and out of the room—I don't even know where to tell you to find us."

"Trust me, I know how to find people in a hospital."

"It's not the best time for you to meet them, that's all."

"So tell them I'm a friend—you don't have to explain your whole life to them. A doctor'll sometimes talk differently to another medical person, even if it is just a lowly nurse. At the very least, I'll be able to translate for you."

"They're doing everything they can already. Christ, they're doing more than they should."

Maggie doesn't say anything.

"Let me think about it."

"Fine. Think. What hospital is he in?"

"I said let me think about it. I'll call you."

"Cath—"

"I'll call you. I promise."

Cath hangs up and stands by the phone, half expecting Maggie to call back, but the phone doesn't ring. She tells herself this isn't what matters right now, her family's what matters, but her mind keeps picking up the argument again. In the middle of her shower, suddenly she's clenching her jaw and telling herself Maggie has no idea what it's like.

Cath has no idea where the words appeared from. What *it* does she have in mind? Her father dying? Her father dying without having read some part of her mystery? Without her having told him she's a dyke? Would it help if she whispered the news in his ear now that he can't push it away? She could sneak it in between the jets of air the machine pumps into him. He can't push that away either.

Cath turns off the faucets and runs her hands over her hair, pressing out streams of water. She dresses, dries her hair and makes herself a slice of toast, then knocks on her landlady's door to borrow a shovel, explaining about her father, about last night's snow, about her parents' sidewalk. It feels false somehow, as if she were playing a role: dutiful daughter helping out in a crisis; isn't she admirable?

By the time Cath gets back to the hospital, her uncle's in the waiting room, sitting between Charlie and her mother, looking like he's been there all night, too. He's gray, diminished, a lifetime older than he was on the day he told Cath that her mother'd been happy to have a girl. Cath pulls up a fourth chair, and they go silent so she can ask, "Any change?"

They shake their heads.

Cath's lost track of whether no change is good or bad. He's no worse; he's also no better. More than she's afraid of him dying, she's afraid of him coming only halfway back, with a mind that's not the same one he had when he left them, with a body that can't do anything on its own.

Her uncle pats her hand and says he's glad she's here, "You and the big fellow over there, both of you." He nods toward Charlie. Some part of Cath begins the old complaint: She was here earlier and longer; she stayed here all night; no one ever pays attention to what she does. She notices the complaint the way she'd notice a TV playing across the room with the volume turned down.

"Have you been in to see him?" she asks her uncle.

"I only got here a few minutes ago."

Cath turns to her mother.

"You want me to call?"

"It hasn't been an hour, but go ahead and try them, sure."

The nurse says they can go in, and Cath tells her mother she'll wait—even if they can get by with three people, four's pushing it.

She calls Maggie from a phone near the elevator. The man who answers puts her on hold, then comes back and says she's with a patient. Cath leaves her name, the name of the hospital, and the letters ICU. Overnight she's become an insider—she doesn't need the full words. As soon as she hangs up she wants to call back and tell him it's important, can he promise that Maggie will get the message or does she need to check back.

Not that asking would reassure her.

She adds hiding Maggie from her family to the list of everything she's done wrong in her life and rides the elevator downstairs to buy a newspaper. While she's there she browses through the magazine rack and looks at the flowers in the cooler—skinny bouquets of daisies, single roses padded with fern and baby's breath, each cluster wrapped in cellophane. The list of things she's done wrong plays through her mind in more or less random order—which means not in their absolute order of importance. It gives a lot of play to her calling a client by someone else's name because it only happened yesterday and because the client she was talking to and the client whose name she used are both black. She's not sure how it happened: a couple of wires that crossed in her brain; a patch of racism lying inside her like black ice on the highway, impossible to spot until the tires lost their grip. She'd blame it on her father being in the hospital, but he was fine then. She fell all over herself apologizing, but she doubts that fixed anything. For all she knows it emphasized it. There's nothing to do now but live with what happened. She pays for her paper and heads toward the elevator before her mind churns up anything worse.

By the time Cath gets back upstairs, Charlie and her mother and uncle are back, sitting exactly where they sat before.

The waiting room serves three units, and it's filled up since the morning. Each family gathers a group of chairs, turns them inward, and keeps its conversation low.

"Any change?" she asks.

They shake their heads.

Cath sets the paper under her chair. Her uncle tells her again that he's glad to see her here. She smiles and tries to look pleased, the prodigal daughter returned, except he has no idea how prodigal, and she hasn't been anywhere. He says it means a lot to her mother at a time like this, having her children with her. Cath shifts in her chair. She supposes this is true; she supposes it should make her happy, but she feels nothing. From the corner of her eye she sees Charlie looking out the window at the south wing of the hospital. She holds her smile as long as she can, then lets it fade.

"It means a lot to your father too," her uncle says. "He knows you're here."

Cath's throat tightens, and she shakes her head, not to disagree, just to release the tightness.

"You'll have to take an old man's word for that."

Cath scrapes her chair back and crosses the waiting room faster than she meant to. In the far corner a woman and a teenage girl look up, and by the door a man's eyes follow her over the top of a library book. She locks the door of the women's room behind her. She's willing to cry here, but now that she's alone nothing inside her wants to do that anymore. She throws water on her face and dries it.

Her mother's watching for her when she comes back, drawn to any sign of weakness like a shark to blood. Or maybe what she's drawn to is vulnerability. Cath isn't in a mood to sort one from the other. Whatever it is, her mother never had much of it herself, but she expected it in a daughter, and she still wants it. Cath stiffens. If anyone touched her right now, she'd shatter. She sets her hands on the back of her empty chair like a politician standing behind a podium.

"I asked a friend who's a nurse to stop by this afternoon. She thought she could get some information for us, or interpret what we've got."

Her mother's face sharpens. She sees surgeries they haven't told her about, tubes, medications, machines that can spin time backward and reconstruct the damaged heart. Charlie's face shows a spark of interest too, but it's a different kind. He understands how important contacts are, and influence, and networks. This is a pure interest; he doesn't have to expect anything to appreciate them. Cath has a value he wouldn't have predicted.

"I'll tell you this about the doctors," Cath's mother

says to Cath's uncle. "They'd have been just as happy to let him die. God help the person who doesn't have someone to fight for them."

"It's all about money," Cath's uncle says. "They cut corners anywhere they can."

"Well, they're not cutting any corners here, I'll tell you that much for free."

Cath's still standing, chin out like she wants an argument. She sits and tips her chin toward her breastbone, but she can't shake the feeling that it's jutting forward still, doing whatever it can to provoke someone. Her mother leans close and puts an arm around her shoulders, shaking her lightly.

"Go ahead and cry if you want to," she whispers. "You'll never have a better reason."

Cath pulls away.

"Mom, leave it, will you?"

"Whatever you want."

Her mother doesn't sound angry. She sounds like whatever's wrong must be wrong with Cath because she hasn't done anything to account for it. She turns away from Cath and refuses to say anything else. The rest of them slip into an embarrassed silence, which her uncle finally ends by saying, "You know, Charlie, I've been having a lot of trouble with my brakes lately. You know anything about brakes?"

"Not much. I know they stop the car. At least, I know they're supposed to stop the car."

The way he says this makes it man talk — bluff, good natured, not a confession of ignorance the way it would be if Cath said it.

"Well, mine stop the car all right, but they make the most god-awful noises when they do it. Not all the time, just here and there. And never when I take it in."

"That's the way it always works, isn't it?"

Their uncle gives an inventory of the times he's taken the car in, and what the mechanic tried and how much he charged for it and the times when he didn't charge.

"I guess I'll just have to keep taking it in," he says at the end of the list.

"Might ought to try the dealer."

"I don't know. Gets expensive, taking it to the dealer."

"Gets expensive taking it anywhere."

The conversation trails off. Cath should offer some topic from her own life to keep them talking, but her car's holding its own, and the rest of her life is a fog right now—she can't think of anything worth mentioning. With a fingernail on her right hand, she cleans the fingernails of her left. Charlie pats his pockets for the cigarettes he gave up years ago. Their mother stares at the doorway.

"Why don't you two get some lunch?" she says after a few minutes, her eyes indicating Cath and Charlie. "Let the old folks visit in peace."

Cath glances automatically at Charlie and sees that he agrees, although his face doesn't give any outward sign.

"What can we bring you?"

"Just coffee."

Cath's about to argue and reads an invisible signal from Charlie: Don't worry about it, we'll bring her something anyway. She has no idea if he's really thinking this, or if she's imagining it.

"Uncle John?"

"Whatever they have. Nothing with onions, though. I can't take onions anymore."

He puts the flat of one hand on his chest, just below the throat.

Cath follows Charlie out of the waiting room. Her mind shows her a snapshot of their parents' house, exactly the way it stood when she drove up this morning, snow lying clean on the front walk, only the mailman's feet marking a trail across the lawn from the neighbors on the south side to her parents' door and on to the neighbors on the north. Her father would have had the snow shoveled and the walk salted before he sat down to breakfast. Then he'd have knocked the snow off the shovel, wiped it down with a rag, and hung it in the garage, inside the painted outline on the wall. Cath doesn't understand how someone who once played jazz could have ended up being this fussy, but the only musician she can compare him to is Frankie, who isn't typical of anything.

"Did you ever hear Dad play his trumpet?" she asks Charlie.

"Why? Does he still have it?"

They're watching the elevator doors, waiting for one to open.

"I don't know. I was thinking about him giving it up, that's all. About whether he missed it."

This isn't exactly true. What she thought was that he gave it up when Charlie was born, as if it were

Charlie's fault more than hers — as if, before their parents had even wrapped a diaper around him, they saw some flaw in Charlie's character that would tear his life apart if he were raised as a musician's child. Rearranging the thought leaves a ripple in the flow of her words, but Charlie doesn't seem to hear it. He gives her one of those older-brother looks that come from a distance she'll never cross.

"He wasn't getting anywhere with it. He was probably glad he had a reason to quit — you know, the kind of thing that keeps you from having to say, *Well, I busted my ass, but it didn't work.*"

A bell chimes behind them, and they wedge themselves into the elevator, joining a flock of people Cath doesn't really look at — they're reasons to stop talking, nothing more. She's never thought of her father as a failed musician, only as one who couldn't make a living at it, or not the kind of living he was willing to raise a family on. It shouldn't surprise her that Charlie sees those as the same thing, but it does — it surprises her into a gaping absence of thought.

On the ground floor, they follow a corridor toward the coffee shop.

"You'd think he'd have kept playing, though," she says. "If he liked music, you'd think he'd have kept playing."

Charlie shrugs. He understands success and failure and all the gradations in between. He understands money and plans and the rational place for their mother to live. He understands sports. What he doesn't understand, he doesn't see the point of, and it doesn't make sense to talk to him about it. And for no reason Cath can see, this thought allows her father to make sense to her: Once you've played for an audience, and once you've been paid for it, you can't just go back to playing in the basement. The hope goes out of it, and the pleasure follows.

She walks faster than she would if she were alone, keeping up with Charlie, moving left to pass a bone-thin woman in a lab coat, moving back beside Charlie once they're in front of her.

"How are you holding up, anyway?" she asks.

"I could use some sleep. I'll be all right."

This isn't what she was trying to ask, but it's close enough. Information isn't what she wanted anyway, just contact. They follow a line of people into the coffee shop, past stainless-steel shelves, plastic-wrapped food, a cash register. Most of the tables are filled now. The noise of talking and the scraping of chairs echo off the walls and ceiling and crash back in on them. The gentle couple with the sweet roll is gone. At the next table are three office workers in their twenties. They're talking about their plans for the weekend, and their voices are hard-edged and cheerful.

Cath peels back the seal on her sandwich and extracts it. It's a pale egg salad on light brown bread, and it's cool and soft in her mouth, all texture and no taste.

"Listen," she says, "I've got to tell you something."

Charlie has his own sandwich open and looks up from stirring his coffee. The voices around them overlap, and the words lose their shape and meaning. Cath hadn't planned to say this and searches her mind for some bush-league revelation to pawn off on him.

"My friend who's stopping by? The nurse?"

At some point she's looked away from him, and she's staring into her coffee now. She looks up.

"The thing is — " She runs her hands through her hair, says "Shit," and folds her hands in front of her on the table. "Listen, you're not going to like this, but I'm going to say it anyway. I'm a lesbian."

Time slows down. Invisible lines spring to the surface of her rib cage and gauge the vibrations in the room, the sound level at the next table, the power of her words to override the office workers' words and force them to hear what she's just said. These are lateral lines, like the ones fish use to communicate, to orient themselves, to sense danger. *A system of distant touch*, her college textbook called it. Evolution is instituting one of its miraculous changes in a species, right here in the hospital coffee shop.

"Yeah," Charlie says, "I pretty much figured that."

At the next table, a woman says, "I know, but he could have called," and then her voice goes under, over-lapped by other words, other thoughts. Cath's mind reaches back and reassembles Charlie's words, first as sound only, then as meaning.

"You knew that?"

"I wasn't positive, but yeah, I thought so."

"You shithead."

They burst out laughing as if this is what they've been holding back all morning. The women at the next table glance over and look away before anyone can catch them at it.

When Cath can talk again, she says, "Do Mom and Dad know?" She hears the present tense and the plural but doesn't go back to sort them out.

"Probably. I don't know. It's not the kind of thing people talk about."

Charlie's still smiling, expecting her to share this joke too, and she does—her face radiates a three-year-old's pleasure at being in on it. She has a younger sister's rock-solid belief that if she and her brother are laughing together the world's exactly the way it should be, even though stretching ahead of her she can see that he'll never once mention that she's a lesbian unless she brings it up first, and then he won't say anything more about it than he can help. And when the time comes she'll be angry about that. Right now, though, she smiles, and she points at the extra cream containers, stir sticks, and sugar packets piled on his tray.

"Charlie, you shithead, how come you take all that stuff when you don't use it?"

"In case I need it," he says.

His face is open and innocent. He's willing to talk about this, but he can't think for the life of him why anyone would want to.

Unfinished Dreams

It's been almost a week since the funeral. On Maggie's side of the bed, the clock reads 12:31, the numbers glowing clear and red through the dark. Maggie rolls over in her sleep and tugs at the quilt, which has slipped off her shoulder. Cath covers her, then presses the flat of her hand against Maggie's back, hoping to borrow its warmth, its quietness, but her mind circles back to the funeral anyway.

What she's thinking is that she should have worn slacks. She hadn't worn a skirt in so long, she had to go out and buy one, and wearing it left her feeling like someone else went in her place, or like she was there but was sleepwalking. She can't find the right image for it and shouldn't try. It's only going to keep her awake.

She pulls her hand away from Maggie and rolls over. A bus rumbles past, rattling the windows. Cath decides it's the last one but doesn't really know. She's grateful not to be waiting on a cold corner, wondering if it's come and gone already. In the dark she sees a sudden picture of the fake-grass rug that was supposed to hide the dirt beside her father's grave. Raw earth and rocks had spilled out under its edge and mixed with the snow. This reminds her of the coffin she should have tried to talk her mother out of because it cost too much.

The deluxe model—the kind that makes up for everything you missed out on in life. It had everything but cable TV. She sighs out loud and turns back toward Maggie, who's making a soft popping sound with every breath.

Cath sits up and pulls on Maggie's extra bathrobe. It's chenille with raised flowers, and it looks great on Maggie. On Cath it's short in the sleeves and too fussy, but Maggie's plainer one is tight in the shoulders, and Cath still hasn't bought an extra one to hang in Maggie's closet. She keeps thinking that sooner or later they'll make up their minds to live together, and when they do she'll have a bathrobe she doesn't need. She feels on the floor beside the bed for her socks and leans against the wall to pull them on.

Trina's at her father's for the weekend, and Cath pads into her room and curls up on the bed, pulling the trailing edge of the cotton spread over her. The shades are up and the room's washed with the eerie bluish white of an almost full moon. Over the course of the week, Trina's spilled her clothes everywhere and thrown her dolls in an unsentimental heap in the corner by the door. A coloring book lies open on the floor, with the dim shapes of crayons scattered around it. The crayon box is nowhere in sight.

Cath grew up believing that mothers—all mothers— saw everything their children did and got mad at them if they didn't put their toys away. She believed that each crayon had to be put back in the box before another one could be taken out. Looking back, she thinks she spent her childhood trying to erase every trace of herself from the house. The invisible child. She can't come up with a convincing argument in favor of this, but Maggie and Trina still send her into shock sometimes. She wonders what Trina will be like as an adult. The problem with having Maggie for a mother is that she'll be damn near impossible to rebel against. Trina gets to wear pretty much what she wants already. If she wants to shock anyone, she'll have to slice off her earlobes, pierce the skin between her thumb and forefinger, or wear heels and frilly dresses and devote years to planning her wedding.

Cath's cold and throws the spread off to open the heat vent, then folds the spread back over herself. She doesn't want to get under the covers. Trina'd never know she'd been there, but Cath would have when she was Trina's age. She'd have known by the way the blankets were tucked in, by the alignment of the pillow, by a rearrangement of the air.

Cath draws her knees up and wraps the skirts of the robe over her feet and legs. It ought to be comforting to lie in a child's bed, but it's not particularly. It's warmer than the couch, that's all.

The problem with being a child, she decides, is that you never get to know the people your parents were before they became your parents. Exhibit A: If she'd grown up hearing her father's trumpet rising from the basement in a long, sad solo, it would have given a name to the loss at the center of his life. They might all have been happier.

This isn't a simple longing. If Cath had grown up this way, she's convinced that his music would have lost its power for her. She'd have rolled her eyes and told her friends not to pay any attention, it was just something her father did — it wasn't important. She believes that wanting matters more than having, that absence is more powerful than presence. She believes that children assign themselves their parents' unfinished dreams, and that his dream of being a musician gave her an edge of restlessness. Without it she'd be a different person — someone she wouldn't recognize; probably someone she wouldn't like.

She asks herself if she'd trade her writing for this change in her history and pushes the question away without answering. No one's offering her the choice. Her father is forever as she knew him, a tired man who liked mysteries and TV cop shows, who went to bed early and staggered off to work when it was still dark. He wanted an orderly life and a house that was quiet after nine. She's not sorry about who he was, only about not having known that other person too.

She pulls the other side of the bedspread from between the wall and the bed and flips it over the first side.

She could at least have asked her father what it was like when he was with the band.

Even under both edges of the bedspread, Cath's freezing. She unwraps herself and pulls the bed away from the wall to smooth the spread into place, erasing every trace of her passage, and crawls back into bed beside Maggie. The clock reads 1:23. She fits her body into Maggie's and waits for Maggie's heat to migrate north. Maggie's as tight about heating the house as she

199

is loose about everything else. Spending a weekend here is like spending the winter in a tent. Cath doesn't see how she can ever move in.

And for this loss, quietly, so she won't wake Maggie, she cries.

Evening

Cath moves though the first floor of River House pulling shades. The house is rich in windows the same way it's rich in woodwork, in fireplaces, in hand-me-downs, in almost everything but money. At the last community meeting, the residents argued for almost an hour about whether the shades should be pulled at night. A couple of the women didn't feel safe with them up, and some of the men felt hemmed in with them down. The discussion branched out into other things: personal safety, personal grudges, the temperature of the water used to wash the dishes. In terms of the residents feeling ownership of their environment, it was a success. In terms of decision making, it was a swift pain. Cath still doesn't know if the shades should be up or down, and Lynn, whose shift she's taking tonight, didn't leave instructions. Not enough residents are around to vote one way or the other, and Cath decides to make her mistakes on the side of safety, even if the connection between safety and shades in the common areas is a little hazy to her. You please a few of the people part of the time and try not to worry about it. It's called compassion fatigue. It's not terminal, but it's not one of the qualities Cath likes herself for.

The only person in the living room is Denise, who's

stranded on the couch like a sailing ship a week and a half after the winds quit blowing. From the shelves on the far side of the room, Denise's three-year-old smiles out of a framed picture, bright eyed and many braided. She has a lopsided grin and a lacy dress. She lives with Denise's sister.

"You mind if I put the shades down in here?" Cath asks.

Denise shakes her head without bothering to answer.

Denise's demons are depression, her sister, and the courts, who won't let her have her daughter back. It's not a good sign to see her sitting this way. She'd been doing well. Fairly well. Not badly. Cath runs through the checklist in her mind, trying to isolate the concrete action, or lack of action, that's bothering her so she can flag Denise's case manager. The best she can come up with is "appears depressed."

Cath pulls the last shade. Whatever safety they offer is in force now — the magic circle's complete. The world is outside and Denise, who either doesn't have an opinion or does but won't say what it is, is inside and safe, her depression heavy on her shoulders and her daughter beaming out at her, reminding her how happy life is someplace else, when she's not there.

Cath retreats to the office and fills out papers — for every client a forest of forms has to be printed, filled out, filed, sometimes even consulted. She makes notes for the next scene of the mystery — Greg Sexton forcing himself to see his mother — but can't settle down enough to write it. Through the vacant rooms between them, she feels Denise weighing on her lungs. The completed forms in the file cabinets press on her too, each folder another life, another history of pain, abuse, illness, disaster, some inflicted on the client and some by the client. In each life the balance is different; what they have in common is that they're clients, so someone's paid to keep score. A record of successes and failures, but the failures always outweigh the successes. They seem like endings, and the successes are as fragile as newborns. They leave years open for failure to try again.

Seven Things

On a rack between the supermarket line Cath's chosen and the next one over, the cover of a women's magazine hypes an article on new spring hairstyles and one on the seven things you should never say to your child.

Cath inches her cart forward enough to catch sight of her own child—her semi-child; her semi-stepchild. Maggie's child, now Cath's underage roommate. Trina's riding on the bottom rack with her knees up like a go-cart driver.

"You okay under there, kidling?"

Trina gives her the barest of nods. Today's Saturday, and normally she'd be with her father, but he got the flu and begged off this weekend, promising every kind of reparation he could think of. The change has left Trina withdrawn and ready to say no.

Why did they only come up with seven things? Cath makes a list of her own: God, you're dumb; that looks hideous on you; I never wanted kids anyway; your brother was never this much trouble; you'll drive me out of my mind one day; you're as bad as your father; this is all your fault—you know that, don't you? She could go on. The world's awash in things not to say to your child. This confirms her belief that women's magazines are stingy.

The man ahead of her unloads his cart onto the belt. Six frozen dinners, half a gallon of milk, a loaf of bread, a bag of oranges, one squeeze bottle of mustard, and a jar of generic strawberry jam. He has white hair and a slight tremor in his hands. He smiles at Cath, then bends farther than he needs to and waggles his fingers at Trina. Cath can't see Trina through the mound of groceries they've collected, but she must be ignoring him, because he straightens up and gives Cath a what-can-you-do-about-it shrug.

Cath's mother used to make her say hello to people who talked baby talk to her, to people who scared her for reasons she couldn't have put into words even if she had understood them. She can see why a child would be insulted by the way this man waved, but she's sorry Trina can't overlook it. She smiles and shrugs back at him, the same adult, what-can-you-do shrug that he gave her. She nudges her cart forward enough to bring Trina's back into view and a wave of gratitude sweeps through her: for Trina's presence in her life; for Trina's mother's; for the casual warmth of a stranger shrugging at her in the supermarket; for not having to buy frozen dinners and strawberry jam. Her smile transfers itself seamlessly from the man to Trina's unknowing back.

The line chugs forward a notch. As Cath unloads her cart, Trina emerges, section by section, divided into squares by the mesh of the basket. Not only doesn't she look up, she doesn't look sideways at the candy display. This impresses Cath; self-denial is the heart of a good sulk. The line moves forward. Cath pays for her groceries, bags them, and loads the bags into the cart.

"Better climb out of there."

"Why?"

"Because of the cars in the parking lot. It's too dangerous."

This comes to Cath as easily as if she'd spent her childhood memorizing it. She has no idea why riding on the bottom of a grocery cart should be more dangerous than riding inside one or walking behind it, but she believes it is, and now Trina does too—enough so that she doesn't say, *My mom lets me.*

"Just to the door, then. I'll get off at the door."

Cath pushes. She tries to find a single phrase that sums up artificial danger so she can add it to the list of things not to say to her semi-stepchild. Will she grow up with an irrational fear of grocery carts, or parking lots, or being wheeled around by brown-haired women? Will she grow up with an irrational faith in authority?

At the door, Trina crawls out from under the cart and walks beside Cath, one hand on the cart as if she were pushing it, although she's not. The wind's cold and Cath pulls her gloves on. It may be time for spring hairstyles in the world where women's magazines are published, but in Minnesota it's the ass end of winter.

"What are the things you think parents should never say to their kids?" Cath asks.

"Get into bed right this minute."

"What else?"

"I want you to take one bite of that. You don't have to finish it, but you have to take one bite."

Trina makes her voice into a perfect imitation of Maggie's, only smaller and farther up the scale.

"Anything else?"

"I don't know."

She says this without stopping to search her grievance banks. Either they're empty, she's tired of the subject, or she doesn't trust Cath with the real stuff.

"My mother used to tell me to smile more," Cath says. "If there was ever anything that made me not want to smile, it was being told to."

She looks down at Trina but can't tell if she understands what this was like.

"She said I'd be pretty if I smiled more. So I thought I was ugly because I didn't, and everybody thought it was the end of the world if a girl wasn't pretty." Cath laughs. "I looked like what I looked like, whether I smiled or stuck my fingers in my ears. She could have saved us both the trouble."

Trina gives Cath an appraising look.

"You're okay."

For a second time, Cath's overwhelmed with gratitude. Not because Trina's made her think she looks any better — her looks aren't bad enough to scare the horses, but they're nothing the girls lose sleep remembering. Or the boys, for that matter. What overwhelms her is the graceless goodness of this child wanting to make things right for her, all these years later. She pulls the shopping cart to a halt at the trunk of her car.

"You're okay yourself, short stuff."

Trina shrugs. Cath unlocks the door for her and wonders about the phrase *stuck my fingers in my ears.* Maybe it was an adaptation of *sitting around with your finger up your nose* or *with your thumb up your ass,* and some mental filter transformed it into the kind of thing you could say to a child. She wonders if it sounded odd to Trina.

When they reach the house, Cath hands Trina the bag with the paper towels and toilet paper. She brings the others in herself, making three trips, lining the bags up on the back porch, then hefting them through the open door while the dog gets underfoot and heat pours out into the late-winter air. She sets the bags on the counter. They'd be easier to unpack if she could set them on the floor, but she can't remember which ones have the chicken, the turkey hot dogs, and the cheese, and she doesn't want the dog snuffling through to find them.

The dog was Cath's idea — a reason for Trina to feel she gained something when Cath moved in. He's a sweet dog, reddish brown, part retriever and part mystery, but he's food crazed. He's sitting at the base of the counter, head tipped up to watch the bags in case one of them suddenly hurls itself to the floor, and he's not about to leave until the last one's folded up and tucked away.

Cath rumples his ears and says, "Gus," and he wags his tail but keeps his eyes fixed on the bags. Trina's in the living room. *Give me a hand putting the groceries away* isn't on Cath's list of things never to say to your child, but she doesn't yell it out to Trina. She unbags celery, graham crackers, and pretzels and puts a second plastic bag over the one the celery came in so it won't go limp in the refrigerator. This is a trick of her mother's, one of the hundred thousand things that has to be done to keep the world from dissolving into chaos.

There must be seven things you should never say to your parents: You know, I *really* like sex. Did you ever have v.d.? You never wanted kids, did you? Guess what, Mom, I'm gay.

Cath's already said the last one, and it absolves her of having to finish the list. In spite of which she knows the next entry: I wish you'd let Dad die in peace. The idea behind the list has expanded somehow. It's not just ugly stuff now — the kind of things other people say because they're not thinking, or they don't care, or they've reached the end of their rope. It's collecting entries that matter; truths that might clear the air; truths that can do nothing but hurt; truths you live with like a stone in your belly. How does the body react to a foreign object it can't incorporate and can't reject?

To make room on the shelves for the graham crackers, Cath pours the tag end of a box of cereal into a plastic bag and sets it on top of the full box. Unless she can slip this remnant into Trina's bowl when she's not looking, Cath'll end up eating it herself. Trina doesn't trust food if she hasn't seen the box it came in. She was fed health food when she was little, and it scarred her for life.

Ninth thing you should never say to your child: Eat that; I fixed it the way you like it. Cath remembers looking at a piece of dead-white fish lying on her plate and wondering how her mother knew she liked it that way when she, Cath, couldn't find the faintest flutter of liking for it anywhere in her.

Maggie gets home from work around three. She hugs Cath, yells hello to Trina, who's upstairs, dumps her jacket on a chair, and throws herself full length on the couch.

"My head's killing me."

"Want an aspirin?"

"I took an ibuprofen at work."

Cath doesn't get headaches and thinks the difference between aspirin and ibuprofen is the kind of technical knowledge only a nurse would have. She accepts the answer as an unnecessarily elaborate form of no.

"Want me to take Trina with me to my mother's?"

Maggie levers herself upright.

"Let me see if she wants to go."

"She won't. I'll tell her you feel rotten and she's going with me, end of discussion."

Maggie shakes her head.

Tenth thing you should never say to your child.

"It's not that bad," Maggie says.

Maggie comes downstairs with the news that Trina wants to stay home. Cath is sitting on the end of the couch where Maggie's feet rested a minute ago.

"You want me to try?"

"She'll be fine here. If I get desperate, I'll let her watch TV, and I'll hide upstairs."

"It's your headache."

Maggie stretches out on the couch again, depositing her feet on Cath's lap. She's abandoned her shoes somewhere — at the top of the stairs, under the pillow, in the freezer. Sooner or later they'll show up again. Cath strokes the sole of one foot through its cotton sock. Maggie has narrow feet, with high arches.

"I saw one of our ex-residents on the street as we

were going into the supermarket," Cath says. "She was so loaded she was reeling."

Maggie grunts.

"Bright woman," Cath says. "I was sure she'd make it."

Maggie grunts again—the kind of sound she makes when she's not listening but knows she should be.

"You are a mess, aren't you?"

"It'll pass."

Cath lifts Maggie's feet and arranges them so the weight sits more comfortably on her legs.

"We should invite your mother over here one of these days," Maggie says.

"She won't come."

"So we'll have asked."

"I'll think about it."

Maggie lifts her head an inch off the pillow.

"Just once when I suggest something I'd like it if you said yes."

Cath lifts Maggie's feet and stands up. Seven things you should never say to your lover.

"I said I'd think about it."

Maggie closes her eyes and says, "I know."

Cath pulls her jacket out of the closet and shoves her arms into the sleeves. Trina's school backpack is half buried in junk on the closet floor and Cath sets it on the chair beside Maggie's jacket, where they stand a running chance of finding it on Monday.

"This place looks like a war zone. How can you live like this?"

Maggie opens her eyes.

"It's not that bad. What I was thinking is it'd be easier for Trina to get to know your mother if she came here. It'd feel more natural to her."

She says this as if they were having a conversation, not an argument.

"I'll think about it, okay? I'll think about it. I don't know if she's ready to do that."

Maggie nods as best she can with the couch cushion behind her head. She closes her eyes. Cath zips her jacket.

"You want me to pick up a pizza or something?"

"I just need some time is all."

Cath takes this as another form of no and realizes she's cataloging these so she can spit them back the next time Maggie complains that she doesn't say yes enough. It's delicious, knowing her arguments are tucked away and ready for her, but she suspects there's a difference between her no's and Maggie's. She suspects she should admit this. Out loud. To Maggie.

Seven things you probably should say to your lover but don't plan to.

She calls good-bye from the door and lets herself out into cold sunlight.

At her mother's house, Cath rings the bell and waits. Before this latest cold spell, the temperature had been hovering on the border between freeze and thaw, and the snow on the front lawn has pulled back from the walk, leaving a border of brown grass. What's left of the snow is pitted and crusty. Her mother doesn't answer the door, and Cath rings again. She imagines heart attack, stroke, death from melancholia and widowhood. She has a key to the house somewhere — the same one she's had since she was ten — but she hasn't used it since she moved out. And she's not sure where she put it when she moved in with Maggie. That's Maggie's influence. Or Maggie and Trina's both. She rings the bell a third time.

Her mother opens the door wearing a zippered bathrobe, blue with rose trim. Behind her glasses, her eyes are puffed and tired. Age has slipped between the skin and flesh of her face, leaving Cath with the feeling that the mother she knows is withering away below the surface somewhere.

"I was in the back," she says. "I wasn't sure whether I heard the bell or not."

"Were you asleep?"

"Lying down. C'mon in the kitchen. I'll make us some coffee."

The living- and dining-room curtains are drawn against the afternoon sun. Against any kind of sun. It's dusk in the underworld. A sharp smell comes from no place in particular, and every flat surface is piled with newspapers, coffee cups, unopened mail: You may already be a winner. It's nothing that would alarm the board of health, but it alarms Cath. She wants to ask if her mother forgot she was coming, but there's no way to say it that doesn't sound accusing.

Cath follows her mother into the kitchen. The curtains here cover only half the window, and they let in a filtered, northern light. Cath drapes her jacket over the back of a chair and watches her mother make coffee.

She moves as if she were under water—each motion slow and heavy. The orange cat pushes his forehead against Cath's leg. He's built like a prizefighter, broad and muscular, and he pushes head-on. He won't be happy until he's shoved her out of his way.

"Mom, has Moe been missing his litter box or something?"

Her mother sets down the coffee filter that she has, with infinite patience, separated from a stack of filters. Cath turns her chair toward the counter, stretches her legs out, and stuffs her hands in her pockets. This keeps them from grabbing the filter, putting it in the machine, and making the coffee herself. Moe repositions himself and rubs his whiskers against the edge of Cath's shoe.

"Missing his litter box?"

"Like hitting the wall or the floor or something instead?"

"Of course he hasn't. He's a good cat."

She picks Moe up and lowers her head to his so their noses almost touch.

"Aren't you a good kitty?"

Moe climbs from her arms to her shoulder, crosses behind her neck, and jumps to the floor, and from there he jumps to Cath's lap. He's like all the Rahvens—he can touch, but if he's going to be touched, he wants to choose when, where, and how.

"Maybe I should change his litter, then. I can smell it."

Her mother pauses in the middle of counting spoonfuls of coffee into the filter.

"No you can't."

"Mom, I can. I smelled it as soon as I came in the door."

Cath's mother pours water into the coffee maker and flips the switch.

"You're imagining it."

"Okay, fine, I'm imagining it."

Cath strokes the cat. Her mother sets cups on the table, cream and sugar, spoons, paper napkins, every item a separate, slow trip. Finally she brings the pot over and pours, then sets it on the table where it can cool. Cath pulls her chair around to face her mother's. Her mind scans all the possible topics of conversation and comes up empty. Long seconds drift past.

"Trina's dad has the flu, so she's with us this weekend."

Her mother stirs sugar into her coffee and doesn't answer. Cath pours cream into hers. Their spoons tink against the sides of the cups. Cath licks her spoon clean and sets it on the table.

"I'm going to get an ice cube for this," her mother says, nodding at her coffee. "You want one?"

"This is fine."

"You'll burn your tongue one day drinking it like that."

Cath's mother pads to the refrigerator. She's wearing crocheted slipper socks, blue to match the robe. When Cath lived at home, her mother got dressed as soon as she got up. They weren't a lie-around-in-your-bathrobe kind of family. They weren't the kind of family that made coffee in slow motion.

"I wondered if maybe you'd want to come over for supper tonight," Cath says to her back.

Cath's mother runs water over the ice tray to loosen the cubes.

"Tonight's not really a good night."

She carries a single cube back to the table, pinched between her thumb and middle finger, and drops it into her coffee. Moe digs his claws into Cath's leg.

"You know sometimes when they miss their litter boxes it's because they have urinary-tract infections."

"That cat's fine and so's his litter box."

Cath holds her hands up like someone trying to show she's not armed.

"I'm sorry. I'm sorry."

She sips her coffee. The ice cube in her mother's coffee is a sliver floating on the surface of her cup. Cath's mouth remembers the taste of cold coffee and sends a shudder down her back. She picks up her cup and sets it down again.

"It's not like you to let things pile up is all."

She nods toward the kitchen counter—the ice melting in its tray, the open coffee canister, a scattering of plates, spoons, and knives, the coffee filters, the clean dishes piled in the drainer, and the frying pan and spatula dirty on the stove.

"This is me living here, so it's like me."

Cath runs both hands through her hair.

"All I meant was I'm worried about you. I don't know. This isn't how you taught me—"

She finishes the sentence by waving her hand vaguely.

"Maybe I taught you wrong." Cath's mother reaches under her glasses and presses the skin below her eyes as if she could press out age, exhaustion, Cath's father's death. "I don't know anymore. When your father was alive, all of that mattered. Now it doesn't. I make breakfast, I look at the frying pan, I think, What's it going to hurt if it sits there till supper? I look in the closet, I think, I'm not going out, why should I get dressed? You tell me, what does any of that hurt?"

"It makes you feel like you're falling apart."

"I am falling apart. Your father's dead, I should be falling apart." Her eyes begin to spill tears, a quiet leakage that she dabs at with the edge of her napkin. Cath's never seen her mother cry before. They weren't a crying kind of family.

"Mom?"

Cath reaches across the table for her mother's hand and squeezes it. It stays curled and limp on the table, but the other hand, the one with the damp napkin, waves her away.

"Just give me a minute here."

Cath takes her hand back, and her mother gets up, rinses her face at the kitchen sink, and dries it with a paper towel.

"I'm sorry," Cath says, although she couldn't say what she's sorry for. Her mother shakes her head — a no as general as Cath's apology — and fits herself back into her place at the table.

"If I taught you wrong, I'm sorry." She says this formally, as if Cath's been asking for an apology. "You do the best you can at the time with kids. You make mistakes. You never know what's important until it's too late."

Cath wraps her hands around her coffee and locks her eyes on her crossed thumbs.

"It doesn't matter."

This comes out in a whisper. She clears her throat and says it again, louder. When she looks up, her mother's staring into the distance, past the kitchen counter and the wall. Cath looks in the same direction, but her eyes stop at the surfaces, making a list of the things she more or less promised not to put in order.

"Is there anything you do want done?"

"I don't think so."

"Grocery shopping? Laundry?"

"I haven't come apart completely. Anything needs doing, I'll get it done."

"It's just that I'd like to do something."

Her mother's mouth smiles briefly and drops back into neutral, a downturned line Cath doesn't remember seeing before her father died.

"I know that."

She says this gently. Cath gives the lid on the sugar bowl a one-hundred-and-eighty-degree turn, then another to bring it back to where it started.

"You're not going to die on me or anything, are you?" she asks.

"I'll stay around as long as this body holds together, Cathy. Not a minute more, not a minute less."

Cath gives the lid another half turn. She says, "Make it last a while, will you?"

"I don't control that."

"Well, do what you can, then."

Her mother nods.

If Cath were like Maggie, she'd push until they either admitted they loved each other or found something to get mad about. She'd say, *Trina's the closest thing you've got to a grandchild, and I want you to get to know her,* and wait to see how that changed the conversation.

There must be a thousand things not to say to her mother. It's a form of love, this piling up of unspoken thoughts, and seeing it this way makes her realize it's not the only form the human race ever invented. If she wants to, she can go on loving the way she has, and by the time she reaches her mother's age, she'll be so heavy with love she'll sink through North Port's rocky soil and take root in the granite of the Canadian Shield itself.

"About coming over," she says. "Whenever you want to, okay?"

"We'll see."

Cath's mother looks past her, at the wall behind her shoulder.

"We'd love to have you," Cath says. "Anytime."

These aren't the words Maggie would have pushed toward, but Cath has combined *love* and *you* in the same sentence while talking to her mother. This sends a rush of warmth through her, and she smiles and repeats the safer part of what she just said as intensely as if it summed up everything.

"Anytime," she says, leaning across the table toward her mother. "Really."

Comfort

On her way to bed, Maggie carries Gus to the landing where the stairs turn. She lays him on a rag rug and kneels beside him, stroking his back, which is one of the few places he isn't swollen.

"Can't give me a wag?" she asks. "Can't you give me a single wag?"

Cath sits on the step above Maggie, and when Gus can't wag his tail Maggie turns to her.

"Maybe I should stay up with him tonight."

"Come on to bed. He'd rather be alone now."

Maggie gives his back another stroke and follows Cath to the bedroom. They don't say that he's dying, or that he isn't dying, but they both know that's what the conversation's about. They've taken him back and forth to the vet all week for tests, for steroids to stop his vomiting, for rehydration to make up for the water he's lost, the water he won't bother to drink, then yesterday for chemotherapy, which the vet explained would work miracles if it worked at all; he'd seen skin-cancer lesions actually shrink overnight.

"Poor old beast," Maggie says.

She's sitting on the foot of the bed, her hands bunching the tee shirt she just took off. Cath puts an arm around her shoulders. Her hand moves the way

Maggie's did on Gus's back, offering comfort where there's no comfort to be had.

"We should sleep," Cath says after a while.

"Let me check on Trina."

Maggie pulls on the oversized tee shirt she sleeps in and stops at the bed to pull Cath's head toward her the way she might if Cath were crying. Cath sits dry eyed and waits for Maggie to release her.

"You really love that dog, don't you?"

Cath pulls her head back to say of course she does, and Maggie goes to see if Trina's asleep, or at least pretending to be. Cath sits where she is, feeling nothing more than the absence of grief. All the signals that would tell her to move her muscles—to stand up, to get ready for bed—have gone silent. There's no reason to stand up yet, and grief can damn well wait till she's alone and there's no danger of being caught in it.

In the morning Gus wakes her by barking twice, strangely. She pulls on her robe and closes the door behind her to let Maggie sleep. He's not on the landing. Sometime in the night he must have moved himself, and Cath has time before she finds him to hope the chemotherapy worked, and then to dread it, because it doesn't promise a cure, only a few months, maybe a year, before this all starts over.

She finds him downstairs, on the living-room rug. His eyes are small and gluey. She touches the top of his head. The only motion is the fur behind his rib cage stirring with his breath.

She dials the vet. They put her on hold, and she realizes she could have talked to the receptionist instead of asking for one of the vets—all she needs to know is if there's any point to bringing the dog in again. At least in theory she could decide this herself. It's not lack of information that stops her as much as paralysis. She doesn't want to be the one to give up on him. This must be one of the reasons her mother kept her father's body plugged in and breathing longer than it wanted breath. It's simple enough, but she never understood it before.

If she went upstairs and asked Maggie what to do, Maggie would have an answer, but she wants Maggie to sleep—she's been sleeping badly all week, and she looks like hell.

Trina's also been sleeping badly. She won't sleep with the light off; she wakes up in the night, and Maggie has to sit with her till she's asleep again. Cath hears Maggie singing sometimes, quietly, and falls back to sleep as gratefully as if she were the one being sung to.

It's never occurred to Cath to let Maggie know she loves this. The pleasure's like grief—it needs privacy.

Most of the weight of Gus's illness has fallen on Maggie. She was the one who opened his mouth last night and pushed pills into him, holding his head up and his mouth closed, stroking his swollen throat until he swallowed. She's the one who'll have to do it again this morning unless the vet says to bring him in, or unless Cath can make herself do it.

She pulls the phone into the living room, snapping the cord to one side when it catches on a chair leg. Gus's fur has stopped moving. She puts a hand on his back and pushes, trying to get a response. She calls his name. She holds an ankle and realizes she has no idea where to look for a pulse. A woman picks up the phone and introduces herself as one of the vets. She says Cath hasn't met her, but she's been briefed on Gus.

"I think this dog's dead," Cath says.

She half expects the vet to say, *So why'd you call me?* but she doesn't. She draws a breath and says, "I can tell you several things you can do to check, or would you rather bring him in?"

"Tell me what to check."

Cath pinches his toe, then puts a finger at the corner of his eye. The vet tells her to touch the eyeball, but she can't; she touches the inner corner instead, by the tear duct, right at the edge of the lid. She feels for a heartbeat, although she's not sure she's feeling in the right place.

The vet says they can bury the dog themselves or have him cremated. "Either way, you should move him outside," she says, "because in about fifteen minutes various sphincters will open."

Cath sets the phone on the table and goes back to the dog. His ears are matted at the edges with vomit. They haven't had the heart to comb them in the past few days. She runs a hand from his head down his back, then brings the rag rug from the landing, wraps him in it, and carries him out to the porch. She's never carried anything dead before, or even touched it. When her father died, she stood beside him and stuffed her hands into her pockets as if she expected him to reach out and grab one. When mice moved into her old apartment every fall, she set traps and then swept up mouse and trap together, squinching her face up at having to come even that close. But she knows this corpse. She's not afraid of it, not disgusted by it, only surprised that even though she's never touched death before, and even through the rug, she can tell so absolutely that Gus is dead.

She fills a bucket with water and soap and begins to mop up pools of drying brown liquid. It could be blood, or it could be vomit or shit—she's grateful not to be sure. The floor blurs in front of her. She runs the mop back and forth over the boards at the base of the stairs. By the time she can see clearly again the stain's gone, and she moves on to the dining room. Gus covered a lot of distance before he'd emptied himself out and could lie down and die.

She empties the bucket in the basement sink. When she comes back upstairs, Trina's standing between the kitchen and living room, wearing a cartoon-character nightgown.

"Is Gus dead?"

"Just a few minutes ago. I put him out on the porch."

Trina starts to cry. Cath starts to cry. She puts a hand on Trina's shoulder, and Trina pulls away.

"You said he'd be okay."

"I did?"

"Last night." Trina clenches her fists. "You said he'd be okay."

Cath wishes she'd gotten Maggie up; she wishes Trina would cry loudly enough to wake her now. She runs her hands through her hair and sits in the old brown armchair, turning toward the arm so she faces Trina.

"I said he might be okay. It was a possibility. It just didn't turn out that way."

"You promised," Trina wails, and she flees up the stairs.

Cath lets her head fall against the back of the chair and cries. She thinks about Gus's ears and cries harder. They barely had him for half a year. He came from the pound, and they don't know anything about his life before they took him, but Maggie's pieced together a story that involves hardship, deprivation, a lack of love, a close brush with death at the pound, and then rescue and happiness — a family, love, a bed and bowl of his own, all the food he needed, even if no amount could ever be all he wanted. Dickens couldn't have written it better. Cath never believed it — Gus was too sweet tempered to have been treated badly for long — but she believes it now. Completely. After all those hardships, to have been happy for so short a time.

She pushes herself out of the chair and pulls a handful of Kleenex from the box in the kitchen. She blows her nose and stuffs the extra tissues in her pocket. Upstairs Maggie and Trina are talking quietly. Because she can't think of anything else to do, she puts away the dishes in the dish drainer and washes the ones they stacked on the counter last night. She wonders if her hands are clean. Even in the soapy water, they feel like they're coated with something.

When she runs out of dishes, she goes back to the

porch and squats down beside Gus. She half expects him to have moved, but he hasn't. His ear's thrown back so the ear canal shows, and she folds it down toward his chin. It doesn't lie quite right this way either. She can't find its natural position. She strokes his head by way of apology for this, and for sleeping through the night, for talking Maggie into sleeping through the night, for not having adopted him sooner, for not managing to keep him alive longer, for everything else she hasn't done and should have.

Behind her the door opens. Maggie has a hand on Trina's shoulder, and Trina's leaning against her hard.

"It's something none of us could help," Maggie says. She comes up beside Cath, moving clumsily because of Trina's weight against her side. She kneels down, leaving Trina the tallest of the three. She puts a hand on Gus's head. "It's nothing to be scared of."

"I'm not scared."

Without her mother's leg and ribs to lean on, Trina folds her arms behind her. It crosses Cath's mind that no sphincters have opened yet—that there's nothing left in Gus to pour out. She'd like to say something comforting to Trina, or something wise. Something Trina would remember in years to come. Something to release the weight of unspoken words. She has no idea what that would be and starts crying again. Maggie knows her well enough not to touch her, not to act like anything unusual is happening.

"We gave him a good life while we could," she says. "And he's not in any pain now."

Cath's not sure who Maggie's saying this to, but she

cries harder—for Gus, for her father, for everyone she's held words back from or refused to be comforted by. She pulls Kleenex out of her pocket, blows her nose, and says, "God, I hate this." She laughs and notices that in the middle of all this she can laugh, and this makes her start crying again. Trina's hand pats her shoulder.

"You couldn't help it," she says. "It's okay. He knows that."

Ellen Hawley has been the editor, for many years, of *A View from the Loft,* and has worked as a cab driver, a waitress, a radio talk-show host, an assembler, a janitor, a teacher of writing, and an editor. She won a Writer's Voice Capricorn Award for *Trip Sheets.*

Interior design by Wendy Holdman
Typeset in Cochin
by Stanton Publication Services, Inc.
Printed on acid-free 55# Sebago Antique Cream paper
by Maple-Vail Book Manufacturing

More fiction from Milkweed Editions:

Larabi's Ox
Tony Ardizzone

Agassiz
Sandra Birdsell

What We Save for Last
Corinne Demas Bliss

Backbone
Carol Bly

The Tree of Red Stars
Tessa Bridal

The Clay That Breathes
Catherine Browder

Street Games
Rosellen Brown

A Keeper of Sheep
William Carpenter

Winter Roads, Summer Fields
Marjorie Dorner

Blue Taxis
Eileen Drew

Kingfishers Catch Fire
Rumer Godden

All American Dream Dolls
David Haynes

Live at Five
David Haynes

Somebody Else's Mama
David Haynes

The Children Bob Moses Led
William Heath

The Importance of High Places
Joanna Higgins

Thirst
Ken Kalfus

Circe's Mountain
Marie Luise Kaschnitz

Persistent Rumours
Lee Langley

Ganado Red
Susan Lowell

Swimming in the Congo
Margaret Meyers

Tokens of Grace
Sheila O'Connor

Tivolem
Victor Rangel-Ribeiro

The Boy Without a Flag
Abraham Rodriguez Jr.

Confidence of the Heart
David Schweidel

An American Brat
Bapsi Sidhwa

Cracking India
Bapsi Sidhwa

The Crow Eaters
Bapsi Sidhwa

The Country I Come From
Maura Stanton

Traveling Light
Jim Stowell

Aquaboogie
Susan Straight

The Empress of One
Faith Sullivan

The Promised Land
Ruhama Veltfort

Justice
Larry Watson

Montana 1948
Larry Watson